ALSO FROM JACKANAPES PRESS

The Ettinfell of Beacon Hill by Adam Bolivar
A Wheel of Ravens by Adam Bolivar
Darker Than Weird: Fourteen Tales of Horror by John R. Fultz
Really, Really, Really, Really Weird Stories by John Shirley
The Voice of the Burning House by John Shirley
The Miskatonic University Spiritualism Club by Peter Rawlik
The Eldritch Equations by Peter Rawlik
Book of Shadows by Manuel Arenas
The Burning Ember Mission of Helldorado by Manuel Arenas
Not a Princess, But (Yes) There Was a Pea by Rebecca Buchanan
The Withering by Ashley Dioses
Darkest Days and Haunted Ways by Ashley Dioses
I Awaken in October by Scott J. Couturier
Halloween Hearts by Adele Gardner

The **Poems for Halloween Series** by K. A. Opperman:
Past the Glad and Sunlit Season
October Ghosts and Autumn Dreams
At Summer's Wistful End

COMING IN 2025/2026

The Exile and Other Tales of Carcosa by Galad Elflandsson
The Black Wolf by Galad Elflandsson
Light from a Gibbous Moon by Galad Elflandsson
Told by Firelight in Timbered Halls by Adam Bolivar
A Few Odd Souls: The Potentates of Urbille by John R. Fultz
The Leering Surf by David Barker
Nightmuse by Scott J. Couturier

www.JackanapesPress.com

For inquiries about wholesale orders or other questions,
please email us at JackanapesPress@gmail.com

"Emotionally complex, character-driven stories of wanderers, people far from home and far from comfortable in their own skin. Not since Lucius Shepard has a North American fantasist written so deftly about Central America. Braum's superb stories are well worth the read."

— BRIAN EVENSON
Author of *Good Night, Sleep Tight*

Also by Daniel Braum

The Night Marchers and Other Strange Tales

Yeti, Tiger, Dragon

The Wish Mechanics: Stories of the Strange and Fantastic

Underworld Dreams

The Serpent's Shadow

Phantom Constellations (forthcoming)

CREATURES OF LIMINAL SPACE

CREATURES OF LIMINAL SPACE

DANIEL BRAUM

ILLUSTRATED BY
DAN SAUER

JACKANAPES PRESS

Creatures of Liminal Space

A Jackanapes Press Book
www.JackanapesPress.com

Cover art and interior illustrations copyright © 2025 by Daniel V. Sauer

Cover and interior design by Dan Sauer
www.DanSauerDesign.com

First Trade Paperback Edition
1 3 5 7 9 8 6 4 2

ISBN: 978-1-956702-16-3

*This is a book about, and dedicated to,
the spaces in between places.*

Contents

Introduction

Liminal spaces can be defined as the transitional places between where one has been and where one is going. Be that physically, emotionally, or metaphorically. To be in a liminal space can mean that one is on the precipice of change, on the borderland of some place new, or at a threshold of a new understanding.

I write strange tales. Stories I often describe as containing "intentional ambiguities" or where it is not certain if what the characters are experiencing is a supernatural or psychological phenomenon.

Soon after delivering the three long stories in the book to publisher and illustrator Dan Sauer I realized that the three shared the common element of liminality. These stories were full of ambiguity, uncertainty, states of transition, a sense of "in-between"-ness, and of not being fully "here nor there," and thus the title *Creatures of Liminal Space* was born. Our excitement for the project grew and Dan suggested that we expand it.

During the years 2008 through 2011 I had written about 50 pieces of ultra-short stories called flash fiction. For over a decade I had thought they were lost but thanks to the help of a friend I had recently recovered and been reunited with them. From this cache I selected stories that contained a "creature," or a "liminal space," or both to join the book as frames for the three longer stories and Dan's illustrations.

You hold in your hands these fifteen stories and fifteen works of art that accompany them. Dan and I invite you to join us in these spaces in between places, and to meet the strange, weird, and phantasmagoric denizens who dwell there.

—Daniel Braum
April 2025
New York

GREAT SANDY DESERT
AUSTRALIA
WESTERN AUSTRALIA
GREAT VICTORIA DESERT
Kalgoorlie
Coolgardie
Eucla
Nullarbor Plain
GREAT AUSTRALIAN BIGHT
Mt. Woodroffe 4,723
SOUTH AUSTRALIA
Broken Hill
Port Augusta
Adelaide
NEW SOUTH WALES
Bourke
Cunnamulla
Roma
Newcastle
Sydney
Wollongong
Canberra
VICTORIA
Melbourne
Bass Strait
TASMANIA
Alice Springs
Simpson
Charleville
Coral Bay
Kalbarri
Geraldton

Kookaburra

I HAD JUST RETURNED from three months Down Under. And being back, I yearned for all those musical Aussie accents and watching fruit bats high in the evening Queensland sky. Was it my friends I missed most, or the sense of living in a city that had not completely steamrolled nature in order to exist?

These were my thoughts this Saturday afternoon. Autumn had just changed the leaves of my cherry tree to orange but I had the pleasure of taking my god-daughter to the annual Pet Expo.

"Be a good girl and hold my hand," I said to Marti. "They have giant mountain gorillas there, so don't get lost."

"Nuh-uh," Marti said, dismissing the notion as one of my frequent teases.

"B'sides. Grillas are il-leeegal," she said, one-upping me, as was our way.

We strolled through aisles lined with booths peddling kittens in cages, greyhounds on leashes, and every pet supply I could imagine. One booth, for a local sanctuary for injured and abandoned birds, was teeming with rather well behaved parrots.

In a cage quietly sat a squat bird with a large black kingfisher's bill, its white feathers dusted with grey and black.

"See, Marti, that's a Kookuburra."

She liked the name, but the bird did not capture her attention.

"She's from Australia," said an old woman. The way she had so smoothly emerged from the bustling crowd of strollers and families, it seemed she had come from nowhere.

I couldn't get Marti's attention away from the parrots. The crowd's almost angry buzz was wearing on me. More than anything, I wanted to be on the bridge overlooking the Brisbane river.

"So go back," the woman said, as if my thoughts were being broadcast. "Maybe you could find a way to bring me."

"I should. And I'd love to," I said, this time certain I had spoken aloud.

"Who are you talking to, Uncle Dovyd?" Marti asked.

"The nice old woman," I said.

Marti gave me a look that said *not another silly tease.*

I turned to point, but the woman was gone.

The Kookaburra laughed. The gurgling bellow, wholly alien, seemed to stop time.

"Wow, that was that?" Marti asked.

Pungent eucalyptus and tropical humidity filled the expo center, and, for the most ephemeral instant, all was silent before the din of the crowd returned.

Breathstealer

BREATHSTEALER COMES AT NIGHT when the line between what is and what was is weakest.

At first she came to me as a shadowy black cat, waking me in the night, her jaguar weight on my belly, paws on my shoulders immobilizing me. I thought she was an ancient curse I picked up in the deep of the rainforest: a manifestation of a vengeful spirit brought home from a jungle-covered pyramid on one of my long journeys of "self-discovery." Surely she was vengeance incarnate, here because of the sins of my youth, my arrogance and ignorance rivaling that of the conquistadors, a trail of emotional destruction left in the lives I touched. I often woke with Breathstealer pinning me and I was filled of thought of my past transgressions, lovers' quarrels risen to screaming matches, low-blow words gone devastatingly too far, the seething yet resigned look on my true love's, my last love's, face as she left me on the side of the road in the middle of the night. I felt my air, my life, leaving along with all these things.

Later on I thought Breathstealer was a blessing, some angelic incarnation here to reward me for all the pain I've felt. I often woke to find an ethereal woman in diaphanous white hovering near me, misty, gentle, hands caressing me with a lover's grace. Thoughts of things long gone, the secret things, the little moments I shared with ex-lovers and ex-friends, filled me. In the last note my true love, my last love, wrote me, she asked, "Where do all the good things go now; where do I put them?" I ask Breathstealer this now. She only kisses me and I feel my air, my life, leaving along with all these things.

My doctor told me I will die if I don't do something. Not enough oxygen when I sleep. A condition called hyper-this and toxic-that. I only know sleep is troubled. Breathstealer comes to me now in a form I know well. I wake in the night to find something that looks just like me sitting next to me on the bed. It touches my forehead with the back of its hand and all the details go till all that is left are congealed notions of moment, of all the days of all the years; a life boiled down to talking points and topic sentences. I know now Breathstealer is not a curse nor a blessing, and I was born dying, as was each moment that passes.

I sleep better now, still I know Breathstealer comes at night, when the line between what is and what will be is shifting.

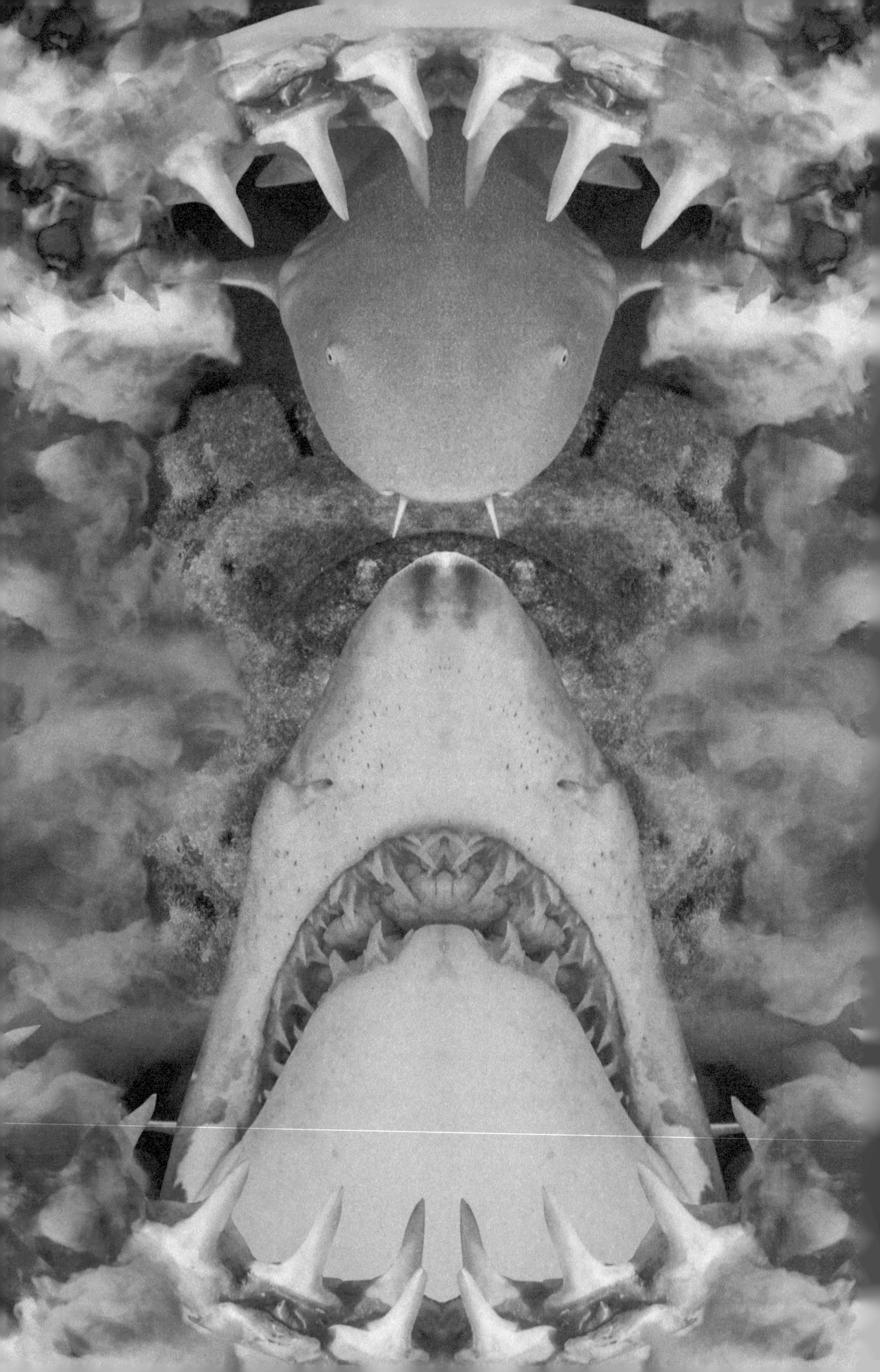

"Go."

"BE CAREFUL," NATALIA SAYS. "The shark doesn't bite, but it's jagged down there."

Her boyfriend gathers her up like a possession. I shrug this off and grab my mask.

It's an eight-foot nurse shark sitting there, motionless, under the broken hurricane wall just like she said. To see it you have to dive about nine feet or so and hold onto the bottom of the concrete, pull yourself down, and hold your breath long enough for your eyes to adjust to the darkness.

The guy next to me is trying to get my attention. Pointing at me. A trail of blood trickles up to the surface. It takes me a few long seconds to realize it's coming from my hand. I must have cut it on the barnacled, rusty piece of rebar I'd been holding on to. Before I let myself go up, I sense the shark is not alone. Something is with it in the darkness.

* * *

That night, I'm in my room, listening to the night sounds of my happy neighbors as I drift asleep. Soon as I turn the lights out, I sense that presence.

My eyes adjust and I see a shark in the corner, standing upright, like a man. It's saying something. All garbled. Lost in translation. But I get the sense it's a command. I turn on the lights and it does not disappear. I can see its jagged teeth and jaw moving as it repeats its command.

My cut hand is throbbing. I look at the bandage, then I'm alone in the room. Except for dozens of ants chaotically fleeing the corner instead of marching to my waste basket in neat lines as usual.

I go outside for air. Natalia is on her steps having a smoke.

"Yoo too," she says. It isn't a question.

"Yeah," I say.

She's leaving tomorrow. I have another few weeks on the island planned. But what about everyone else?

In my head I hear the sound the shark was making. Was it saying, "Go"? My throbbing hand tells me it's a warning.

Where the Jaguar King Lives in the Dark Heart of the Wood

Stann Creek District, Belize. Winter 2011.

IT IS SAID THAT the Jaguar King lives in the dark heart of the wood. Watching over all the cats.

The wood's proper name is the Cockscomb Basin Wildlife Preserve and Jaguar Sanctuary. 150 square miles of tropical forest. All five of the cat species that dwell in Belize can be found there. Jaguar, Puma, Jaguarundi, Margay, and Ocelot.

Sunset Rick is an American expat. He runs a two-unit vacation place, Sunset Rick's, in the little beach town not terribly far from Cockscomb. He's at Rosalinda and Enrique Alvarez's farm, which borders the Eastern edge of the preserve, picking up his order for the week. The predawn sky is still a glistening carpet of stars, illuminating the clearing where the Alvarez's vegetables are growing. Rick looks to the jungle, a living wall teeming with layers and overlapping layers of buzzing and clicking that looms over the farm. He walks to his pickup truck, bags of produce and dairy in hand, and scans the shadows and spaces between tree trunks for motion.

The guests due in to his second cabin, June and Andy from New York, are arriving in the afternoon. The thought of flying, even on one of the puddle jumpers that are the only planes that land on the air strip, reignites a little flower of unease in his beer-gut belly. It has been decades since it has been his job to keep one of those rumbling metal behemoths in the air. Circling to and from the fail-safe points, day in, day out. Armed with a nuke and extra fuel. And it's been decades since he crashed the little plane he had here out in the jungle, the last time he ever flew at all. He's grateful for the fragrant smell of wet earth and flowers and green and the hint of smoke from someone's trash fire in the damp almost-morning air. A morning doesn't go by that he does not at least think about kissing the ground and small swatch of beach where he's made his home. He doesn't tell guests the Air Force was where he got the name Sunset Rick. He doesn't tell guests he knows how to fly at all. He does tell them he spends his time drawing and watching for birds. And for big cats, if he's lucky. He's always on the lookout. Jaguars are tough, if not near-impossible, to spot. Most visitors and locals alike will never, ever see one.

A shape moves across the Alvarez's field. Black on black. Just a shadow? Or is something there? He knows the jaguar he calls Cygnus likes to venture out from Cockscomb during the night to rummage in garbage for easy pickings before returning at dawn. Rick holds still and squints and yes he sees her, right where the green jungle meets the farm. She's there. Just inside the line, just inside the boundary of the preserve. Where it is illegal to harm her, illegal to shoot any jaguar. She's trotting along, openly, brazenly, not concealing herself as she is so capable of doing, as if she knows the boundary and knows the rules, somehow. Maybe she knows he'd never, ever even think about shooting her. Maybe she knows Enrique Alvarez would love to blast her. As would several others who live nearby who do not share his awe and appreciation. These people think twice before shooting. Not only to be sure their quarry is outside the border. They know Sunset Rick isn't the only one watching. They've heard the stories. The Jaguar King is out there. Watching over the cats. Protecting them. Even avenging them. Rick has been here twenty-plus years, one full year before Cockscomb was founded, and while he has his notions, he can't say for sure if all the stories are true. He's also never seen a jaguarundi; yet he knows that doesn't mean these most reclusive of the cats are not real.

Cygnus halts. Turns her head and looks Rick's way. She can smell him. Knew he was present long before he had any hint of her. Rick wonders if she's contemplating the Jaguar King too.

A raucous toucan call, the first sign of day, punctures the night-time cacophony. The jaguar bounds off, her spots and sleek feline contour becoming one with the tangle and brush as she flees the coming morning for places where daylight cannot reach.

* * *

June and Andy watch as the little Cessna, which they and their luggage deplaned from just a minute ago, reaches speed and lifts into the air at the point where the dirt strip of a runway ends at the Caribbean Sea. Sunset Rick is watching them from the shade of a rusty tin roof held up by four poles at the corners that is the "airport."

He swings open a hinged section of the rusted remains of something that once upon a time was a barrier and says, "Welcome."

Andy doesn't like the way the old expat looks June up and down as she's hunting for her smokes, but he's used to it. She's in a T-shirt with Duran Duran's *Rio* album cover on it, half tucked into a pair of black denim cuts offs. Bruises from iron-deficiency, in various stages of fading, mar her pale legs. Her short shock of hair that was once punk during the days when she purchased the T-shirt remains short now for efficiency not style. Endless hours at the shop and time with her niece and every iota of sleep is what counts, though she feels she cleans up nice on the date nights Andy every so often persuades her into. She lights up a clove cigarette, a real one, contraband Andy provides for her, somehow, even though it has been years since Obama banned them. Andy doesn't want her to smoke, yet he keeps her flush with them because her money is tight and he knows how much she loves them. She takes a big pull, inhales like her life depends upon it, then realizes the men have already loaded the luggage.

The three of them fit easily in front of the truck. The windows are down. Belize's heat is palpably real; the November snow and all the crushing minutia they've left behind is a ghost unable to dwell in it.

"First time here, you two?" Sunset Rick asks.

"I come to Belize a lot," Andy says. "Well, used to, back before I met June, I mean. Never made it this far down. Always wanted to. I told myself I would, one day, you know, come back with the woman I love."

"Good old love and romance, I remember that," Rick says.

"I remember it too," Andy says. "This one… protested, but she's here. We made it."

June smacks Andy's tattooed bicep.

"I run a business. And have… a daughter," she says. "All I need right now is to be eaten by a jaguar or get some tropical disease."

Rick reaches down with one hand, his other never leaving the wheel, and produces a can of beer. He glances at Andy and June to see if they will dare to voice disapproval.

"Yeah, we do have jaguars," he says. "Scarce on diseases though. Plenty of beer. Want one?"

"Can I smoke instead," June asks.

"Sure."

He swigs his beer just as they hit a patch of bumps.

The road is an unpaved swath cutting through untouched jungle on both sides broken up only by the infrequent clearing or sign indicating the presence of one of the few area businesses.

"A paved road is on the way. Supposedly. Someday it's really gonna come. Along with cops. And rules. Well, real ones. For now, we're still free here, though. *For now*. There's no AC in the cabins. You'll want to get the ceiling fans going and—"

"It's perfect," June says.

Rick sees her face light up as she takes Andy's hand.

"It's absolutely perfect here. I see what you mean," June says. "You were right. I *can* see myself staying here forever."

Andy is painfully aware she didn't say "*us*." A small thing, considering all sign of the nicotine starved, sleep-deprived, uptight, worried bundle of nerves he spent the long day of travel comforting has disappeared into the tropical heat and sun.

"Why the change of tune, sweetheart," Rick asks.

Andy braces for June to blast him for the patriarchal endearment. But no. There's only that faraway look on her face. The one she wears when she's in the place she goes when in the grip of her lowest lows, the place he can never reach her.

"There's a jaguar," June says. "Nearby."

"What?" Andy asks.

"I can… feel her. I… see her spots. She's almost all black, you can just make them out. You see her when she moves, then she's gone into the jungle like... oh I don't know how to say it. We have to find her. I have to see her."

Andy and Rick exchange an inquiring stare, each expecting the other to offer an explanation.

"I guess this means we're going after all," Andy says. "I knew there was a reason I loved you."

"I'm down for going right fucking now."

"Easy cowboys," Rick says. "You don't have to go far to see a jaguar.

We've got one around here, exactly like the one you described. Damn if I know how you did that. Hell, you near picture perfect described the jaguar I call Cygnus. She comes out of the preserve every night. Why they get a taste for our garbage is beyond me."

"Andy's always wanted to go. That's why he planned this whole trip, to take me."

"You heard the lady."

"Is there anywhere around here we can rent a car?" June asks. "Or, maybe do you think we can use your truck?"

"You're my guests. After you lovebirds settle in, I'll do my best to be of service."

Rick knows the Jaguar King doesn't like outsiders. He wonders what's he gonna think of these weekend-warrior-hipster-has-been-wanna-bes. Stupid question. He knows the Jaguar King doesn't care for humans, at all.

* * *

The two guest houses at Sunset Rick's are right on the beach. Separated by a lush, greenery-lined walkway winding through the property to the house by the road where Sunset Rick lives with his wife.

Andy has come because he is thinking of asking June to marry him. He hasn't asked yet. Partly because he believes she'll never go for it; after what she's been through, she's said she'll never belong to a man or anyone, ever again. And partly because he's told himself the only time he'll ever surrender to love again is when he finds a woman who'd live out his dream with him—a dream of going far enough south to find the jaguars—a dream of finding a place to stay forever, like Sunset Rick has done. For the longest time this standard insured he'd never love and thus never could be hurt again. He knows he's been running from himself, with Belize being the place he runs to most. To lick his wounds. Collect himself. To find himself in connections and companions made on the road. In travel families he hoped would become families for real yet always crumbled. So many of his hopes always seemed to be going south—to find jaguars. He always yearned to be southbound himself and for a family for real. One that swould last.

June is here because she hates herself. The self she's become. She hates pretty much everyone, Andy just less so than most. She knows Belize is where he used to run away to. She's not sure if it was running from the law or something in his head or his own kind of Peter Pan syndrome. She knows something about running away. When her sixteen-year-old daughter overdosed on pills and almost died she lost custody to her piece of shit ex. It wasn't that she let Anna-Lisa use, she just didn't police her; she didn't think pot and pills was a problem. Javier didn't police her either. Three months into living with him, Anna-Lisa was drunk behind the wheel, learner's permit in pocket. The crash killed her and two of her high school friends. And then Javier was out every night. Her so-called friends saw him all the time in his restaurant in Astoria and never failed to report back about how nice and how popular it was. Did they think this was supporting her? She knows what Andy doesn't—that you don't have to go far to run away. Most of the time, she is just… numb. From the work and hours keeping her studio afloat. And when there isn't that, there's Andy. He's kind to her. He wants her, sometimes it seems like he worships her, sometimes it seems like he even listens to her. Surrendering to this kind of numb is new, sometimes she thinks maybe it could be something real and she's learning how to be good with that.

She knows it's *not* good that Andy's always running away, at least for now he wants to run away with her. These little islands of time he steals with her, sometimes feel good enough; at least as good as all the other intoxicants she's ever tasted.

* * *

Andy is asleep five minutes after they fuck. She is glad for the sex, which back home often falls victim to the stress and the fighting and the catastrophe de jour. When they are fucking she feels alive. Lit up, everything ailing her just a shadow. She watches him, his hand on the little notebook he scribbles drum notations on, post-sex, as he often does. She understands the drain of the travel has sapped him yet this leaves her alone with her thoughts— the last place she ever wants to be. At least she can smoke in peace without his disapproving silence. She flips through the guest book on the kitchen counter. Line after line of names of happy couples and how much they enjoyed their stay. The only one of interest reads: "Going to Cockscomb? The best guide is a quarter mile up the road from the Alvarez farm— Frankie and Ivy." She dresses in a sarong and goes outside. The sound of gentle waves a hundred yards away greets her along with the tang of marijuana on the air. She ducks onto the fern-lined walkway covered in trees and plants of all kinds and flips open her pack of smokes.

She trips. There's a fat black power cable on the ground she didn't see. It originates a few yards away, plugged into a shiny red powder-coated generator. A bearded man in a beefy, mechanized wheel chair is tending to it, a wrench in one hand, a smoking blunt in the other. A small black house cat watches from the safety of a cat carrier at one side of his chair. A square oxygen machine on wheels with plastic tubes is on the other.

"Watch your step there, neighbor," the man says.

"That you? I smelled you from my cabin."

"Guilty as charged."

"Something tells me Mister Sunset Rick doesn't mind you and your cat smoking up in his garden. He's so cute. Can I pet him?"

"Oh, my cat doesn't partake. His name's Larry. It's not safe around here for little ones—"

"So, no petting, in the carrier he stays," a female voice says.

A tall woman with a mane of jet-black hair is walking towards them on the path. She's cool and collected, dressed in a black tank, black capris, and worn-in Doc-Martens. June is immediately conscious of the fact she's a sweaty mess.

"I hope his smoke isn't bothering you," the woman says. "He always smokes when he is setting up."

She has a European, accent—Russian, maybe? A bass guitar slung on her back. June hates her already because she's thin and fit and half her age. Pretty as hell without a stitch of makeup. Two sleeves of bright, colorful tattoos she would kill to have. The kind of woman she knows Andy fell for before her.

"We were just getting ready to play," the woman says.

Is she blowing me off? June asks herself.

"Um… don't mind me, I'm just having a smoke. Then jaguar hunting, hopefully."

The woman kisses the man on the forehead. "You got this?"

"Yeah," the man says. "Go. I'll have you powered up in a jif."

"Ciao," the woman says.

June watches her walk to the beach, playing her bass as she goes. A half a mile off the tranquil shore there is a tiny island. Crowded with palms. A wooden ship, an old one with sails, is anchored off it. June ashes her clove.

"Want one?"

"Nah, bad for the lungs. Want some of this?"

"Hell yes," June says.

The man hands her the blunt. June takes a deep pull, then glances at the oxygen machine, confirming it is off.

"That your ship out there?" June says, exhaling a mouthful of smoke.

"I can neither confirm nor deny. A real beauty though, right?"

"Really? Okay. Who the hell comes to Sunset Rick's with their cat? *And* a generator. Guitars. *And* the boat from a CSN album cover?"

"It does look like that one, right?"

He tells her their names. And the name of their band. She doesn't retain a word. She recalls giving him a fake name. She wants nothing to do with the person she is back home. Those ghosts have caught up to her and all she can think of is *how did her life come to this*. And how jealous she is of this guy and his girl.

"…we were staying a bit up the coast at Francis Ford Coppolla's hotel. Not. Recommended."

"Copolla's place? Sounds fancy."

"I don't mind fancy. I can get used to fancy. Staff is not cool. Who doesn't like music? You and your man like music, right? Rick's place is the best."

June worries that the sleep she was so looking forward to has just gone out the window.

"Rick does seem cool," she says. "I think he's going to lend us his truck."

"Right. You said jaguar hunting?"

"Yeah. Not hunting-hunting, but yeah."

"Rick told you about Cygnus?"

"He did."

"He must like you then. Don't let his shit-talk about the Jaguar King give you pause."

"Jaguar King?"

"As in, fuck with the jaguars the Jaguar King's gonna come and get ya, Jaguar King. Big black jaguar? The jungle boogeyman?"

"No. Nope. Didn't say anything like that."

"No?"

The man motions for his blunt back and takes a hit to break up the uncomfortable pause.

"Oh, never mind. They're just stories to scare people. Jaguars are so… exquisite. Aren't they? Obviously, you agree. I know you do. Probably why I like you already. Cats, I have to say… are most important to me. They're not to be trivialized, not to be fetishized. Or forgotten or used and abused. Sunset Rick knows this too."

"Shit, don't know if that means Rick likes me or not after all."

"Ah, he loves ya. Now, I gotta get Natalia her power going. Things might get loud, you said you two like music…"

"We do, but… what the fuck?"

The man gently places his wrench and blunt on the ground.

"Come here a second, please," he says.

"Uh, I gotta go."

Larry the cat gives a tiny yelp.

"Aw, no, we're cool. I gotta tell you something, quiet."

June cautiously steps closer. When she's a few steps from him, he speaks.

"The "fuck" is, this is for Natalia. She… doesn't have a lot of time."

"Oh," June says.

"Oh, is right. This is what she wants before she goes." He gestures to the ship. And the generator and the two amplifiers on the dock at the beach where Natalia is plugging in. "So, this is what she gets."

"Oh, listen, I'm really sorry."

"Don't be. It's been a good life. When it's time to go, it might as well be here, right?"

He puts the blunt out and returns the oxygen tube into his nose. There's static, then a single, deep bass note reverberates from the shore.

* * *

Marcus S. Nelson was a biologist from New York who specialized in big cats. His friends called him "Markie." Every summer for most of the 1980s he'd come down to the Cockscomb Basin, working on the wildlife corridors and big cat territories with the people who went on to found the preserve. The year before the preserve was founded, he hired a local pilot to fly him over the area to fine tune the map of the terrain. The small plane hit the tree tops and crashed in the jungle. The wreckage is still out there; no one had a reason or the resources to cart it away. Markie's body was never found. And he has not been seen since.

* * *

June parks Rick's pickup on the dirt road just outside Enrique Alvarez's farm. The sun is almost down. A group of a dozen Mayan women are walking to the road trying to keep in the shade. Andy's leaning on the truck eating an obscenely big American-style burger they picked up at the beach bar down the road from Sunset Rick's. The women are trying not to, but they cannot help but stare at the two newcomers, out of place with their new clothes and tourist food.

Where the road turns onto the farm it narrows to barely one car-width wide. Rick told them the guides live and run a visitor center not far past the Álvarez's, just inside Cockscomb.

"Will you let me drive?" Andy says. "The going looks rough."

"It does. That's why I'm driving."

Andy puts his trash in the back seat. A rifle is there on the floor. He says nothing of this as June drives into the jungle. After a few hundred meters, the trees and vines meet above them, covering the road in a canopy alive with birds, and motion, and insects and butterflies that flit back and forth between outbursts of white flowers. The air is moist and heavy. Full of pollen and musk and loam, yet undeniably… clean. Andy spots a couple of chickens and a rooster strutting towards the farm. He fingers the ring he has concealed in his shorts pocket.

"June. You know I love you, right?"

"Um, yes dear," June says and laughs. "What do you want now?"

The roar of a motor and chug of unmuffled exhaust breaks the dusk-time lull. A huge, dirty truck is barreling towards them on the road ahead. June pulls the wheel, sending the truck off the road and into the forest. Andy slams against the passenger door as the other truck steam rolls past without stopping. A trio of men, rifles slung on their backs, sit in the open bed, grasping the rusted side for hold. For the first time ever in Belize, Andy is frightened.

"What the fuck was that?" he says.

June tries to back up, but the pickup's wheels spin. June throws it into drive and the truck moves forward, rumbling over ferns and saplings and brush onto an embankment sloping into a stream. An animal trail leads into the forest on the other side. June stops and inhales deeply.

"Hey wait a sec," Andy says. "Over there, what's that?"

On the trail on other side is an animal walking towards the stream. It's twice the size of a large house cat, with a super-long tail. Its center of gravity is low to the ground.

"Is that an otter?" Andy says.

"Looks like a … weasel. Only … bigger."

The animal halts and looks across the stream at them. It has a cat's head. Dark gray fur.

"That's not a jaguar."

"No way," Andy says.

The thing rolls on its back, exposing its belly.

"Damn trusting thing, whatever it is," June says. "All that noise didn't scare it off. It must like us."

"Likes you, my dear," Andy says.

The stocky, cat-like thing pads to the water and takes a long drink. It looks across the stream at them again then turns and pads back on the trail into the trees.

* * *

The odd beast is on their mind when they roll up to the lone wooden building in a clearing a quarter mile up the road. There is a satellite dish atop the high roof. A hand-painted wooden sign reads "Welcome Center."

June is eager and knocks while Andy is still in the truck putting on bug spray. A short Mayan man opens the door. Inside is a single large room, with a high thatched ceiling and a fan moving the air around, a layout common to the area. There are two long picnic-style tables that appear intended for guests. A woman and a child sit at the far end of one of the tables. A flat screen is mounted in the corner near them, showing a weather report. Another younger child is in front of a laptop computer at the other table.

"Hi," June says. "We're the two that just called an hour ago. No one answered. We also sent an e-mail. About going into Cockscomb."

"I am sorry," the man says. "We are about to have dinner."

"Would after dinner be okay? We've come a long way."

"It has been a long day here."

"For us too. I gotta tell you," June says. "And to top it off these guys in a truck pretty much ran us off the road and we saw this thing down at the stream like a big cat-faced otter. Any idea what that was? You live around here—"

"Jaguarundi?" the woman says and comes to the door.

She ushers June inside and to a poster on the wall that shows drawings of the five cat species that live in Belize. She points to the picture of the jaguarundi.

"Oh, jaguarundi, yeah, that," June says. "I never heard of it. We're here to see jaguars."

"You saw a jaguarundi? Now? Where?"

"At the stream, just up the road. Not more than ten minutes ago."

"I have lived here seven years and not seen one yet."

"She's lucky when it comes to cats," Andy says from the doorway.

"Why do you want to see jaguars?" the man asks.

Anna-Lisa's face in the emergency room blooms in June's mind. All blue and air-starved. The stale air of her dark room fills her, the taste of oil and chemical and sweat, and the tired hum of outdated equipment running down the years. Compassionless voices of people she knows slur into one drone about their days, their husbands, their fabulous lunches. The crack and the ring the first time Javier's hand met her face follows. And her body's memory of how good and how awful it felt to punch him back.

"I just have to see one," she says, softly.

She's conscious of how ugly and loud she must seem to have come knocking at this hour like this. That's not the woman she wants to be.

Andy has his wallet out and open. She doesn't have the words to stop him. He's always been generous to her; it is his way. For once, just once though she wishes he would let her handle things and that she had the words to express this without rage.

The woman takes the money from Andy.

"Okay, wait outside. Until we come for you," she says. "After we put my children to bed my husband, Sam, will take you."

* * *

Sam is barely as tall as June, who stands at about five six. His face is round; a little moustache beneath his sloped Mayan nose. June's not sure if he's older than she and Andy, yet she recognizes he moves with the deliberate gait of the elderly, the overworked, and those preoccupied with a great burden. Something she knows too well. He retrieves a tree branch from the damp path for a walking stick, turns on his long flashlight and leads the way into the jungle.

After an hour with him, she likes that he is quick to smile and thinks his pensive eyes are kind, but she can't stand it that he ignores her when she says she hears things in the jungle on either side of them. Andy hasn't outright shushed her but has asked her to stop bothering the man and it is maddening that neither male will listen.

"This is the part of the forest where the secondary growth ends and the old growth, the primary growth begins," Sam says. "The trees in this area have never been cut. You can see they are bigger. With more space between them. The battles for sunlight have been won and lost long ago."

He taps on a bark-covered vine as thick as his arm that is wrapped around a fig tree wide as a small car.

"In an emergency you can cut this and find water," he says.

The vine spirals around and around the tree and all the way into the dark heights above where bats flit in arcs and tight turns chasing insects that the humans do not see from the ground.

A six-foot-long black snake, thick as the vine, slithers onto the path a few paces ahead. It rears up, tastes the air with its tongue, then resumes its journey across the path, disappearing into the trees.

"What kind was that?" Andy asks.

"A fer-de-lance," Sam says.

"That sounds poisonous," June says.

"It is," Sam says. "Do not be afraid. If you see a snake again, get behind me."

"Afraid, fuck no," June says. "I'm kicking myself I only have my phone with me. Getting ready, things were so crazy. I didn't even pack my camera. Are we going to see it again?"

"Let's hope not," Sam says.

Andy wonders what getting behind Sam is going to do. Does he kill snakes with that stick? June's pre-trip concerns about coming here that he dismissed as no problem are back in his mind.

"I think I hear something," June says. Again.

"The fer-de-lance likes to take sleeping birds," Sam says.

He walks to a tree with low hanging limbs and points to a bird sleeping in the leaves.

"Some do not sleep in nests—they just sleep. Sometimes snakes and owls take them."

June marches in front of Sam and points.

"Out there to our right," she says.

Sam shines his light to where June has pointed.

"A peccary," Sam says. "You might call it … a big pig."

"How do you know?"

"The eyes," he says. "Look there."

He shines his light in the ferns and plants. Hundreds upon hundreds of pink and orange dots are illuminated in his beam.

"Every animal's eyes are different. They all respond to light. Those are spiders."

June and Andy shine their beams at the low greenery too.

"Those are all spiders?" Andy asks.

"Yes," Sam says. "Every one of them. If we find a jaguar, I will tell you to turn your light off. Some animals freeze. Jaguars do not like it."

Andy bends to fix his laces. A small brown snake is curling its way around the tree trunk he has grasped to steady himself.

"That one is harmless," Sam says. "Careful—there are things if you touch that will make you itch."

Sam resumes walking and gestures them to follow. Andy follows a few paces behind, and June a few paces behind him.

After a few minutes Sam stops and bends down.

"Here are jaguar prints," he says. "Fresh. Look. They were made tonight. Here is where a jaguar reached the trail. And next to her was her cub."

June snaps photos with her phone. Sam walks with his head down and stops after a few paces.

"Here is where a big male, wow, look how big, crossed the path. Maybe he was following them. Maybe he wanted to see who was in his territory. Now shine your light that way and look."

There is a shape a dozen or so yards into the forest. At first June thinks it is a car or bus covered in jungle before realizing it is a plane, like the one they flew in on. Smaller trees and vines have grown in and on and around it.

"Long ago, before the preserve was founded, one of the men working to protect the cats crashed here. You can see where we lost the primary growth trees and the newer trees have moved in for the sunlight."

"Do you think it was left here because they were afraid of the Jaguar King?" June asks.

"Jaguar King?" Andy says.

"He's the one who kills you if you fuck with the cats," June says.

"Where'd you hear that?"

"When you were sleeping. I met our neighbors."

"They cool?"

"Do you like music?"

"The Jaguar King. He is not real," Sam says. "A story to protect the cats. How would we take the plane away even if we wanted to? Nature wastes nothing. Given time."

"Okay, I'm not fucking around. I really heard something this time," June says. "Something is out here with us."

"There are many, many jaguars in Cockscomb," Sam says.

"How many—"

"Guys, shut up! There. In the tree."

Sam shines his light where June is pointing. Then immediately clicks it off.

"Lights off," he says. "Off. Turn them off now."

With the flashlights off the darkness is near complete. Andy thinks he's hearing everything sharper. The insect's buzz. The whir of frogs. His heavy breath. The rustle of the jungle.

There's a deep grunt. Then a *chuff, chuff, chuff* coming from the right side of the path, above them.

The noise changes to a guttural growl that sounds… like an annoyed expression. The stillness breaks. Moving air hits Andy's face. Something hits the ground next to him with a solid thump.

His spine comes alive. A place inside reminds him he is prey. That he is meat.

There's a jaguar on the ground. Next to him. Rumbling and growling.

He hears its steps on the moist ground. Hears it breathing. Something soft brushes his arm. Its tail? The darkness explodes into motion, the sound of paws on dirt and broken brush and cracked branches. The jaguar is bounding away. Andy's senses have it pinpointed as it bolts into deeper darkness.

They stand there for a long minute. Listening. There is only the sound of human breaths and the jungle. Andy reaches to hold June's hand. She does not let him take it.

Sam flicks his light on. Andy's not sure if June has been laughing or crying or both.

"…that was probably the big male who's prints we saw. He is gone now. Jaguars are naturally curious…"

He realizes that June is crying. He touches his cheek and realizes tears are streaming down his face too.

* * *

The return hike to the entrance is in silence. Midway, June stops and listens to the jungle. Sam and Andy stop too. When they near the starting place June's stride slows and her eyes go far away. Andy reaches to put his arm around her. She smacks him in the bicep.

"I told you I heard something. It was following us the whole time," she says.

"You were right, you were right," Andy says.

"I wonder what it's doing now," June says.

"The jaguars like it in the center of the preserve," Sam says. "Humans don't go there. The jaguars know this."

"Can we go?"

"It is two days in, two days out. We were lucky to come this close to one tonight."

"When was the last time you took someone?"

"Years ago."

June thinks of the names Frankie and Ivy in Sunset Rick's guest book. Did their moment of vacation bliss last?

"You said you moved here. Seven years ago?" June asks. "Why'd you come? The jaguars?"

An owl passes overhead.

"The jaguars, I like. Yes," Sam says. "I think Cockscomb needs me. No one wants to live here. Especially young people. Everyone good moves away."

"I heard a road is coming," June says. "Do you think that will be good?"

"How does one answer these things?" Sam says. "I don't want here to become like everywhere else. I know change will come, though. And Cockscomb will grow. Maybe it can grow up to be wonderful."

The owl has landed on a low branch. It cocks its head and looks at them.

* * *

Dawn is still an hour away when they pull away from the Alvarez's farm. This is the point in their date-night pattern where they would have sex. No matter where they were. In the back seat. On the side of the road. In the Guggenheim Museum restroom. Tonight, she is glad he is too tired. She knows there is something wrong with him. His energy has been too low and he passes out too much, even for him, and not just from working.

"Promise me you will see a doctor," she says.

It is rare that she says anything. She's asked him so many times she has stopped bothering. She does love him. At least the him that he used to be. The him that he sometimes can be. That he sometimes sort of is. He's passed out and does not hear.

A big green snake crosses the road. It is at least ten, maybe fifteen feet long, its body longer than both lanes. She is glad to enjoy the experience of seeing it without having to filter it through their shared existence.

The sun is almost ready to come up when June parks the truck back at Sunset Rick's.

There's bass and drums coming from the beach. The playing is surprisingly gentle. And not as loud as she had expected. She gets Andy out of the car and walks him to their cabin and into bed.

There's no way she can sleep. Her mind is racing. She steps outside the cabin and lights up a smoke and asks herself if she wants to get high with the neighbors. She decides she does, as she finishes her clove.

She watches Natalia at the edge of the dock, playing her bass, her form just a silhouette in the night. Her man is slumped in his chair, asleep with a guitar in his lap. Rick is in a chair further back. An audience of one. Looks like he is asleep too.

June hears drums. Real ones, yet she does not see a drum kit. The sound is coming from across the water. From the ship. Natalia's long, sliding bass tones and the sparse, deceptively simple, open beat—plenty of room in it—are meeting half way. Blending perfectly with the sound of the waves.

And the sounds of the end of night and the coming morning. It might be the most beautiful thing she's ever heard.

Larry the Cat is out of his carrier. He's on the beach where the dock meets the shore, chasing small crabs.

To June's surprise a jaguar is crossing the sand towards the little house cat. Creeping low and steady. Its lithe form unmistakably female. Black spots barely visible on black fur. This was the one she envisioned when they landed. Neither Natalia nor Larry see it. They don't know it's there. The jaguar rises from its crouch and changes its trajectory, heading for the water away from the humans. Larry notices it and bolts for the dock. The big cat trots into the gentle surf. And into shoulder deep water, then it is swimming. Toward the boat? Toward the Island? Only her head is visible.

June puts the clove out and decides she's going to tell Natalia a jaguar is near and that her playing is beautiful.

There's a man standing a few feet from her in the darkness of the path.

"Holy shit, Rick. You scared the shit out of me."

The man is tall. Old and lean. Long, thin gray hair. No beard. There's some sort of dark ichor or dry blood all around his mouth. He's barefoot. And wearing only tattered remnants of shorts. This is not Rick. This man is feral. His hands are covered in that same dark ichor as his mouth. There's the smell of musk. The smell of the jungle. His long limbs do not seem right; there are long, pink raised scars where bones were broken and improperly set.

June instinctively steps aside to pass him. The man matches her step, placing himself in her way.

"Who are you?" June says louder than she intended. "What do you want?"

She knows she should be afraid. She finds she is only curious.

"I want you to come with me," he says. "You know where."

His voice is gentle and cultured. With a hint of a familiar accent. Erasing the notion June had that he would be mute.

Sunset Rick has heard her. He's up. Crossing the beach. A rifle in his hand. The feral man and June watch him near. When he is a few paces away he lowers his weapon.

"Markie?" Rick says. "Is that you? Are you for real?"

Sunset Rick has not seen his friend since he crashed the plane out in Cockscomb. Since he saw him crawl away, battered and bruised into the dark heart of the jungle that day. He'd always wondered and had his notions of which of the stories of the Jaguar King could be real.

The Jaguar King extends his hand for June to take it. June wonders if it will be hard and rough. Or if her hand will pass through it as if is nothing.

The decision to find out, the decision to close her fingers around his, to follow as he asks, is not a decision requiring contemplation at all.

* * *

June did not return home. When Andy awoke that morning, she was gone. Her possessions in the cabin not disturbed. He has not seen her since. Sunset Rick claimed he had not seen her. He cooperated but was of little help in the investigations that the Belizean police and the American authorities undertook.

Years rolled on.

Some days more than others he thinks of June. He thinks they really could have been something. He's not sure he understands himself fully; he's still a major work in progress but thinks there was a chance he and June could have found themselves, found some meaning, together. They were just finding out about the part of love that is making choices and building something. He doesn't think he's ever going to know about that now.

He walks back to his side door after throwing out his trash, the 3 a.m. sky and cold night uncaring of what he wonders about in quiet moments like these. Something moves at the foot of the driveway. The place inside him that came alive when the jaguar jumped next to him comes alive again. The feeling of being powerless in the night, sometimes so far away, so readily returns.

The sound is the neighbor's cat. It is walking, perfectly balanced atop the plastic fence, leaving the scene of the crime of the knocked over trash can he now has to clean up. June's empty-eyed faraway expression fills him. Sometimes he thinks he can feel her, that she's standing still as she does, with that faraway look on her face, and she's out there, somewhere, somehow, in the dark heart of the wood.

Boon of the Monkey God

THE ROAD TO THE SHORE winds down the mountainside, a narrow snake covered by lush green canopy, alive with birds and butterflies. A troop of monkeys swing above paying us no mind. Our host, ever-present on the shaded porch, is dressed all in white as she cuts pineapple for the kitchen, a Colonial cigarette in her red-painted lips. The hotel room offers nothing but a ceiling fan as respite from the midday Costa Rican heat, so we trek to the beach, and bring along a bag with fruit for the monkeys that live there.

A resonant howler cry joins the song of the lazy afternoon.

"Make a wish," Connie says. "They don't do that during the day!"

"Okay."

"So?" she asks.

"I'm saving it."

She smacks me, playfully.

We're just about at the bottom when a four hundred horsepower roar decimates the tranquil buzz of animal sounds and gently breaking waves. A candy-apple red sports car speeds down the hill, convertible top up. The tinted passenger side window rolls down revealing the innocent face of a pretty Costa Rican teen. She's done up in god-awful make up and is wearing a whore's dress. A man in a dress shirt and tie leans over.

"How the hell do I get to the beach?"

"You can't," Connie says.

"Come on," he says. "*She* wants to see the beach."

His asinine behavior makes me ashamed to be an American.

"No vehicle access," I say. "Cars aren't allowed."

We leave him to spin his wheels, literally, and go for our swim. We move farther and farther up the beach but we can't escape his shouting and revving engine.

"That arrogance must serve him well in his life, but it's not going to do him any good here," Connie says.

Not yet, I think, afraid of what the future might bring.

We take another dip then trudge to our room. A breeze from the waves below blows the thin drapes. I turn the ceiling fan on. Its lazy spin accelerates and then it is rocking in its loose anchoring. We lay on the bed. Kiss. Take off our clothes. Soon we are matching the fan's rhythm.

As sleep takes us, I hear the sports car on the road. A monkey howls. This time I make my wish.

Connie is still asleep when I wake. I go outside to the communal kitchen to find ice cracking in glasses on the patio bar, but no patrons. Our host is gone from her eternal post, lipsticked cigarette still burning. I glance down the mountain to the shore: not a human present in the waves or the beach. A boat, unguided, crashes into the rocks.

A howler jumps from the canopy to the table and joyfully smashes an empty glass. His eyes full of acknowledgement of my selfish wish. I walk back to the room, with a mischievous smile.

"Hun, want to go for a swim?" I call.

Matthías and the Sentínel

CORNELIUS AND MATTHIAS SAT at Flamingo Airport's tiny departure gate with the flock of antsy tourists. Cornelius nervously ate crackers out of the box one after another, while watching a sun burnt family play a game of Yahtzee in the uncomfortable molded plastic seats as if it were the World Cup. A green blur whizzed past the bar where the security guard was standing. Matthias gripped his case tighter and cursed the Buyer. But it was a false alarm—just two American kids throwing their stuffed toys around.

Sedated and wrapped in damp towels inside Matthias's carry-on bag were three baby yellow-headed parrots. The endangered birds were worth a fortune, at least to his buyer. He and Cornelius had come to Bonaire to track down the nests in the secluded North shore of the island. Only seven hundred remained on the planet. Exactly the sort of thing his buyer liked.

Cornelius was one of the best trackers. Matthias had the knack for smuggling. Getting things through customs came naturally for him. All they had to worry about were those things… the Sentinels, the Buyer called them. These days it seemed every animal they tried to move had one of those mystical protectors. Matthias wasn't scared of ghosts. But Cornelius was frayed to his core. Matthias had considered passing on this job. But the Buyer said he'd take care of the Sentinels and he had something big lined up for them after this. He couldn't resist.

* * *

Preboarding for the flight began and Matthias thought they were home free. Then a green blur swooped across the terminal. As it glided toward them it took on the shape of a green parrot. He was glad Cornelius hadn't seen it; he didn't need him panicked.

The parrot hovered in front of his face. At least this Sentinel didn't look so bad. He still had bad dreams about the snakes and spiders from past jobs. So much for the Buyer taking care of things. He braced himself for what came next. Nothing happened. The parrot-sentinel-thing was just hovering there. Like an image stuck on a television screen.

"Something wrong?" Cornelius asked.

"Nope," Matthias said.

He heard the wet rags inside his bag crackle and sizzle. So the concoction and magic words the Buyer had given him weren't bogus.

You came through after all, thought Matthias.

"I'm looking forward to what comes next," Cornelius said.

Matthias liked the look of the parrot-thing, frozen there. Powerless. Taken by surprise and unable to stop them.

"So am I," Matthias said. "So am I."

The Moalaí

~~~~~~

KODA WAS SUPPOSED to have been out hunting for clues to the whereabouts of the ape-man of the forest. Another one of the Americans had come to her village with a television crew and there was money to be made. The day wore on and she found herself deeper in the jungle than she had ever been before. She stopped to rest by a clear pool of water surrounded by lush greens of every kind. As Koda rested, the surface of the water came alive with color. Big fish were jumping, their scales scintillating where the sunlight touched them.

Koda fashioned a makeshift line and hook out of vine and stick and ran it into the pool with the remains of her lunch as bait. After only a moment she had pulled out the most beautiful fish. She hurried home; her previous money-making task eclipsed by this newfound good fortune.

* * *

Koda sold the beautiful fish for a handsome price. She returned to the pool again and again. It turned out no one else in her village had ever seen the pool nor could find their way there, no matter how they tried. Koda's fish, which she called Moalai, were in demand and became a source of fortune. Koda became rich. Her fishing trips to the clear pool were her source of comfort and connection to what was beautiful in the world. Sometimes she even saw the ape-man of the forest on the other side of the pool, quietly drinking or just watching the fish. Over time she was courted by the sons of businessmen and fishermen from the coast. After many years she chose one and had a large family but always returned to the pool once a week to bring home a Moalai.
~~~~~~

* * *

Koda and her family prospered for many decades. One day her daughter asked her if she was still happy. Koda did not answer. On her next time at the pool she did not take a Moalai. She walked farther into the forest, perhaps into the domain of the ape-man. She knew she would never return to her family again. In her mind she answered her daughter's question of "Why?" You love something until you cannot or do not any longer, Koda thought. And then she disappeared into the woods, chasing good fortune.

A Loch Ness Monster Under the Light of the Southern Cross

Staan Creek District, Belize

ONCE YOU'RE DONE WITH the sense of loss and the loneliness and the pain and range of emotions you go through, there is something freeing about not mattering at all, about being no one's number one in this world. It's a release. From all the twists and turns. The patterns you find yourself in. All the things, of your own making and otherwise, holding you in place. Time helps. Some days you still wake up raw and hollow, not from your most recent loss or from any one thing, but from the weight of all of it.

Lena doesn't see this. How could she? Some cuts are too fresh.

There are only a couple of huts here and ours is perfect, stark and empty, a clean slate; the sky, the sea, the jungle, the flowers providing all the color and sound and beautiful things I could want around me.

An elderly lady, dressed for a flight back to New York, is clamoring about the manatee that has surfaced in one of the sink holes on the property and Lena isn't even interested in looking.

I tell the young Belizean guy renting us the jeep that we're headed to Ihaka's down near Placencia and he says, "Just make sure you don't go to the unfinished condos next door."

"Why?" I ask. "Rough parking?"

He shrugs.

"Everybody knows it's the one place you don't go."

The elderly lady stops directing her even more elderly and dazed-looking husband who's rolling their luggage and chimes in.

"Oh, darling, we went past it on our way back from the ruins. Such a shame. It has so much potential. Sleek buildings. Clean lines. Our driver told us it was built by a drug dealer, so now no one wants to buy it and finish the job."

"Didn't he say something about a shoot-out and a suicide?"

"They're such a lovely couple, dear—don't rain on their parade. Love, let me tell you about this place where we had breakfast, perfect for you lovebirds—"

"We're not a couple," Lena replies, flatly.

Like me, she never fit in. With dark eyes and light tan skin from her Polynesian mother and a smooth, clear complexion from her father's Scottish side, she was always too beautiful to be teased. Mostly I remember her as simply… present, a lot like now. Her brother was the one who drew the spotlight. There isn't a touch of gray in her long black ponytail, only a sheen from the sun, and barely a wrinkle on her, unlike so many of the people we went to school with.

"We're visiting her father," I say with a smile. "I've known them since I was a kid."

We aren't interesting enough and we've lost the woman's attention to the task of getting her bags into the airport van. I can't help seeing the vast emptiness in her husband's eyes. That and something about the way he stands says he's… lost… he's… just along for the ride. Despite paying enough attention to know the drug-deal-shoot-out story, he's not really here at all. It's the same with Lena. I don't think she liked hearing her brother's name out loud. I feel the distance between us and between me and everyone. I had hoped for otherwise, but the feeling is nothing new. In the uncomfortable silence I hear the ocean murmuring from not far away, the din of all the living things in the trees, and the call and replies of birds that sound nothing like home.

We hop in the jeep, top and doors off, and I gun it. The heat doesn't seem to bother her, nor the bumpy road. She smells like alcohol and I hope I wasn't wrong about pegging her for being a good traveler. In the fun little airport bar in Belize City, waiting for our puddle jumper, she was enthusiastic about the green cocktails in martini glasses made with pisang liquor. She talked about the war and the stock market with a young couple traveling with their adorable Pekinese, all good signs.

"Glad to be here?" I say.

She only gives a nod.

I immediately wish I hadn't spoken. When someone's mind is in a maze there's not a lot you can do to lead them out.

How long does it take to communicate the events of decades gone by? The scale of disappointments? A day? A week? Even after everything that scarred and didn't heal, I never lost sight of the fact that the world was full of love. I never felt the need to escape. Despite countless ghosts and memories in so many of my everyday places I never felt the suburban streets were harsh or ugly or even painful anymore. No sharp edges. Things just became… worn, and acquired an ever-present weight, unnoticeable on most days. At least the good ones. I was feeling that benign numbness yesterday when I reconnected with Lena.

The road's two lanes carve a path through an incomprehensible mass of wild greenery and trees on either side. I like the heat. And the wind. Lena produces an airplane size liquor bottle, I have no idea where from, and downs it.

In the second my eyes are on her someone darts into the road. I swerve and manage to keep the jeep off the muddy ditch of a shoulder and moving forward. Lena doesn't appear fazed, so I guess she's all right. More people emerge from the jungle. They're carrying something above them. Something big. A dead crocodile. It's huge. They're walking with it in some sort of procession. Belizeans and expats. A couple of dozen people from all walks of life. I slow to a halt to let them safely cross the road.

"Hey, honk for us," one of them calls.

Lena reaches over and smashes the horn, to their delight.

A couple of young men jump on our hood and slap our windshield and give the thumbs up.

"What's going on?" I say over the engine and the people. I can hear they are singing. Something mournful.

"We got him. This is the saltie that took the Johnson's kid, Syreeta," a shirtless American guy with long dreads and baby face tells me. We watch them cross and disappear into the other side. Maybe heading for the beach, I guess. I notice some monkeys in one of the big strangler figs in the tangle of trees just sitting there on a bough eating fruit and watching too.

"They got that thing in the jungle?" Lena asks.

"Maybe in one of the underground rivers? Or sinkholes. This whole area is connected that way."

I get us moving and before long we've reached what I think are the condos. There's a gateway and long drive that looks like it belongs in Beverly Hills or New Jersey leading past a moat-like canal circling the place. The canals and uniformity of the rows of white buildings evoke every gated community in Florida I've ever seen. The road veers right and a big painted wooden sign comes into view. "Ihaka's." Draped in Christmas lights, it no doubt cannot be missed at night.

I roll into the dirt patch of cleared jungle that is the parking lot and line the jeep up with the dozen or so cars there—new and mostly clean, rentals like ours. A few paces inside the tree line I can see the wall-less bar, the bamboo struts and thatch and two shelves of liquor beneath the taxidermy crocodile exactly the same as we saw it on the TV in 7-Eleven.

And there's Lena's dad, shaking a metal shaker. Right out of my childhood memories, same dark glasses and all, not looking like he's aged much. He's in a loose-fitting dark dress shirt and slacks, not the plain gray suits I remember when I used to watch him walk from his car to his front door when arriving home from work. I hadn't put eyes on him since the days the Smiths broke up and left us holding tickets to their show at the Ritz. His son's name on the big sign and Lena's tense stare leave no doubt it's him—as if there were any question.

"You okay?" I ask Lena.

"Mmmn hmmn," she says. "Let's get a drink."

We take seats at the bar. Her dad's still tall and skinny and pasty white. Up close I see there are wrinkles on his forehead and dark patches under his eyes. Lena catches his attention and orders.

"I see you've got Midori. Good. Two melonballs, extra vodka for me. Hold the pineapple juice for him."

For a second I'm clueless, then I remember it was Ihaka's drink, just the way he liked it. He loved those godforsaken concoctions and didn't give a flying fuck if any of his jock teammates rousted him for drinking a "girly drink."

Lena's dad puts a plain brown square of a napkin in front of each of us.

"Two melonballs. Got it. Coming right up."

He turns, grabs two highball glasses from the hanging rack and begins fixing the drinks.

Forget about me. How can it be that he doesn't recognize *her*?

"Fuck this. We're out of here," Lena says and is on her feet.

I know it's been … how long? But not recognizing your own daughter … Lena marches to the jeep. I don't dare say a word.

"Keys," she says.

I throw them to her and hop in the side.

"How dare he use Ihaka's name," she says as we roll past the sign.

She peels out and we're back heading north. She brings the jeep to a dangerous speed then slams on the brakes. She backs up right on the road and turns into the condos.

"Here?" I say.

"I want to see this fucking place," she says.

"It looks abandoned. It is abandoned. Nothing to see."

She parks up against the big gate and gets out of the jeep. There's an access door that isn't padlocked and it swings right open.

I follow her. The path to the row of finished houses is flanked by a canal. The water is clean and flowing, looks like rain runoff draining to somewhere. Hurricane and flood protection, just like Florida, I guess. The canal circles the development and weaves in and out of the buildings. They're a bit weathered but look unused. Unfurnished. No personalized accoutrements I can discern, until I see a little red light in an unscreened window. A trail cam. Its black housing does not look weathered at all. What the fuck?

Lena's at the last house in the row before a big building at the edge of the jungle. She pulls the door open. Of course it isn't locked. She steps inside and I hurry over.

This one is lived in for sure. There's one wall of books, another with ceiling to floor shelves full of bottles, all different shapes and colors. There isn't one, alcohol or otherwise, that I've ever seen before.

"Lena, I don't like this. We should get out of here."

"You're right," she says.

We go back outside. Instead of turning to leave the compound the way we came, she walks toward the big building and takes the path into the jungle. I see sinkholes flanking the path where it runs under the trees.

"Careful," I call. "There could be a croc or something."

She doesn't stop. I contemplate whether I should hang back and give her space or follow.

I check out the large building. I wonder if it was a gym or common area. It has big glass windows—maybe a greenhouse? They're all steamed and it's fogged up in there. Not one of them has been broken.

I follow Lena into the trees.

A couple of hundred yards in, I find her sitting at the edge of a large sinkhole. There are no trees above. The sun is going down. It smells like summer.

The surface of the perfectly clear water captures a reverse image of the vine-wrapped trees and their countless shades of brown, and the lush green fronds and ferns and saplings all mixed in with the rocky side of the sink hole disappearing into the earth.

As I walk over to sit next to her, I startle a foot-long brown lizard with a triangular crest. Rear toes spread wide it dashes across the surface of the water, its long tail disturbing the water lilies. As it crosses the center point its scales shimmer white and pink and green in the sunlight before it disappears onto the opposite bank. I notice petite white flowers on one of the vines creeping around a robust gumbo limbo tree. And there aren't any mosquitos. I can see why the little town was built here; this is a paradise. Lena downs another airplane bottle of rum.

"I know that sucked," I say. "It's okay to be triggered."

"I'm not triggered."

In the quiet of our silence there is the rustle of the air moving the canopy, the din of sounds radiating from the leaves and branches akin to the buzz of New York's cicadas yet wholly new and alien. There's a back and forth of bird calls so full about their business that I am certain that this is their world and we are the interlopers.

After a few minutes, she gives a solid poke to my shoulder and points to the water.

"What?" I say.

She shushes me, puts her finger over her mouth, then whispers, "What the fuck is that?"

"Where?"

"There. Right there in the middle."

I ease myself to my feet.

"I don't see anything," I whisper.

There's only the crystal-clear water. Not even a ripple.

She can't hide her disappointment and stares at me as if I'm crazy. I have the feeling this expression is one I would know well should the trajectories of our lives keep us together after this. It is the reciprocal of her sated face, the one I saw seconds from sleep and still flush with heat in my bed last night, her disheveled hair transforming my pillow to a thing of beauty while I told her things not only were going to be all right, they were going to be amazing.

It's been one hell of a long day, an upsetting day and she's probably a little drunk and dehydrated. It was only yesterday I had decided to roll by my childhood home on my way back from the grocery store. To feel something. To feel like anything besides a ghost haunting the places that had sprung up over the decades in the places I once knew. I never would have guessed I'd find myself here today. With her. Feeling alive again just like that, yet still feeling so lost.

* * *

New York. Yesterday.

I ROLLED SLOWLY DOWN the familiar suburban cul-de-sac and parked across the street from the house I grew up in.

And I sat there, thinking.

When you're young you shrug things off. The young keep going, unaware that the amount of pain and loss and disappointment one can bear is a finite amount and that one day you might find yourself wondering if there is strength enough to survive one more heartbreak or if your capacity for love and connection has been worn down to a null possibility.

In the decade since my parents sold it and headed off to fairer shores, I'd made a few visits in order to dwell in my childhood memories. Block-wide matches of Ringolevio. Games of our own invention played well into the dark of summer nights. The Thomsons' house next door.

One of my favorite hiding spots was in their back yard behind their old pool house (there hadn't been a pool since long before they moved in, but Lena's dad used the rickety structure as a shed.) It was great because there were two ways out, and you could also climb the fence into the Siegel's yard and be on Mimosa Court in a snap if you heard the other team coming.

Lena was a year older than me. Ihaka five years older than her. And little Tavish, in my mind forever the baby, at least a decade younger than us all. Lena's mom and dad worked long hours and kept to themselves and thus Lena and Ihaka were always the last to have to go inside for the night. Lena's Mom worked in a flower shop and her dad worked in a liquor store;

we thought they may have owned both businesses but never knew for sure. Her dad would arrive home at odd hours. I always thought he looked grim, marching from his car to his front door without waving to or acknowledging us. We mostly were not allowed inside and had to wait at the door for Lena or Ihaka to come out to play. The handful of times we were allowed in, Mister Thomson was always the one who told us when it was time to leave. One time big-mouthed Chris Eisman asked him since he was from Scotland if he had ever seen the Loch Ness Monster and the question had prompted an angry outburst, the only display of emotion I'd ever seen from Mister Thomson at that point.

Usually, a trip to the pet store was my prescription for being lost in the past but my bearded dragon, Mister Hieronymus, had bit the dust last week. I'd adopted him—more like saved him—from my ex's kid when we split over a decade ago. The lizard was the last nebulous connection to a path long gone. It surprised me how hollow its passing left me. Not because I no longer knew if my ex was alive or dead (and hated that I found I no longer cared either way) or because I figured the kid was all grown now and likely did just fine having forgotten me long ago; it was that this cycle of caring for and shopping for the lizard was at an end and there was now one less thing holding me to the earth. The timeless oak trees against the sky of the old neighborhood and caws of the blue jays, no doubt the descendants of the ones I once knew, I hoped would be a balm.

The door to the Thomson house opened and there was Lena, all grown up and middle-aged and looking divine in a smart black suit, walking out with two people who looked like realtors. I watched them put a wooden "For Sale" post up on the lawn and thought about rolling down the window and saying hello. How long had it been? Thirty-five years, at least. I decided too much time had passed and we were too far from the selves that once knew each other, so I just pulled away and headed for the 7-Eleven a couple of blocks away that used to be the gas station we bought beer at when we were underage.

Cheating on my health routine with diet soda and chocolate was my go-to self-care, self-defeating as it was.

Inside the store, a flat screen above the coffee station blared one of those ubiquitous travel shows. A hostess in a sun dress sampled unreal green cocktails in a far-flung airport bar. I hated that there was TV everywhere.

A flock of kids who didn't seem old enough were mobbing the coffee station, which was fine so long as they stayed away from the fountain soda.

I carried my full cup toward the register, watching the screen despite myself; the hostess, now in a bikini, had moved on to a bamboo tiki-bar in the jungle.

Someone slammed into me, knocking my cup to the floor in a spray of cola and fizz.

"Holy shit, holy shit, holy shit," the woman said.

"Hey, it's okay, it's just soda."

"That's my dad. That's my fucking dad up there."

It was Lena. On the screen it was her dad, Mister Thomson, behind the bar shaking a metal shaker for the hostess. I had not seen him since he left, and from her reaction, neither had she.

"Ronnie? Ronnie Greenbaum?"

Her words were slurred. She was drunk.

"After you went to LA I saw you once on the Jools Holland show and that was it, I always wondered what happened to you."

"So did I," I said.

I thought we were going to laugh but instead we looked to the screen and watched her dad pour drinks beneath a mounted taxidermy crocodile draped in tropical flowers.

"How's your Mom? Tavish?"

It was all I could say. There was no way to put my feelings into words, which were that, thirty years after what happened to your brother and your dad, I still carry it with me, and it colors my every notion of trust and safety.

"It's just me now," she said.

"I'm sorry."

"Yeah, your folks been gone a while now. Holy shit, I never expected to see you but… I'm glad," she said.

"Really, me?"

"Yeah you. You were always kind. You remember that time after school you stood up to all those assholes for me."

"Oh, yeah, was that like in tenth grade, wow. I haven't seen you since… your graduation?"

"No. There was that time I ran into you out East, at the Talkhouse, right before you left for California."

"What? You sure?"

"Oh, yes. I just split from my fiancé and was about to play my first show and was losing my shit in the parking lot. I was about to bail as you were driving up."

"I have zero memory of this."

"Come on. You were so there for me. It's one of the things I'll never forget in this life. You told me how beautiful I was. And how smart I was and that I could do anything. Not just get up there and play that show but anything I wanted with my life."

"I want to lie to you and tell you of course I remember this. But sadly I was probably pretty high."

"You didn't hit on me. You just lifted me up and told me to get myself up there and have the night of my life."

"And you did."

"I did."

"This is the best thing I've heard all day. I'm glad as hell to hear this."

"So. What are you doing here? You're… back in New York. How are you?"

"Um, good. I guess… Feels like a loaded question."

"It isn't."

We laughed.

"I've been back pushing two decades now."

We both looked to the screen.

"What the hell?" I said.

She didn't say anything. She didn't need to. The way she stared said it all. That we thought he was dead or at best that we'd never, ever see him again.

"If we're not laughing we're crying, right?" she said. "You still drumming? Hey you want to catch up over pizza?"

We went around the corner and got slices. The same spot we used to go when we were kids—the name had changed, though. After, she wanted to come to my place to put some flowers and what was left of the hornworms on Mister Hieronymus' grave.

In my living room she told me she'd decided she was going to Belize to see her father now that she knew where he was and asked me if I would come then passed out on my couch with flowers still in hand while I was waxing poetic on whether I should or shouldn't.

I was awakened in the middle of the night by her climbing into my bed. We bought plane tickets online, under the covers. Putting my arm around her felt awkward. She seemed to be right at home curling up against me, though.

"Do you remember that one time when we were kids when we almost kissed?" she asked in the dark.

What could I say about that day? A day I thought of often. A day I never liked to speak about, even now.

"How could I forget?" were the only words that I could find.

* * *

Staan Creek District, Belize

LENA STANDS AND WALKS along the bank, glancing in the sink hole every couple of seconds while navigating the tangle of brush and saplings. What is it she thinks she sees?

"Hey, I think we should split."

"I want to check it out a little more. Will you just give me a few?"

"Ok, a few," I say. "Be careful, please."

I take the trail out and stop walking at the big building. The side facing the jungle is made of two barn-style doors. I pull one open just enough to peek inside. Cool white mist wafts out and the odor of turpentine and something resinous hits me.

I inch my head in and find the large space is mostly empty. Up top, a sprinkler wand running along the row of sunroof windows kicks on with a hiss. Through the moisture and fog I make out a large rectangular table in the center, running the length of the place.

Something big is on it. All wrapped up in bandages. Some sort of animal? It has a long snout like a croc but the thing is not croc-shaped. And although it's the size of a whale, its shape is nothing I've ever seen before. Its neck is … long. Too long for a crocodile. One of the cream-colored medical bandages has unfurled and hangs from a thin, triangular flipper.

I step inside. The air is heavy, even more humid than outside and tinged with a herbaceous smell. Beneath the green and floral odor, the reek of something sweet and pungent lurks. At the far end of the table is a cart loaded with odd bottles, the same different-colored glass we saw in the housing unit.

I take another cautious step and freeze when red lights wink on. More trail cams. I breathe for a moment, staring at the clouds of mist glowing pink, then back out. I catch a whiff of something plum-like and resinous as I close the doors.

* * *

New York, long ago

JUNE SMELLED LIKE ice pops and Band-Aids and lawn grass and calamine lotion and hot asphalt in humidity and the preadolescent sweat of Lena and me and Chris Eisman and all the other kids gathered for the daily game of kickball on the Thomson's lawn. We watched Ihaka, all decked out in a tux, walk to his dad's old sedan cradling a delicate flower in a plastic box instead of his ubiquitous lacrosse stick. He returned inside and reappeared toting a clear plastic bag loaded with two big bottles of liquor, one green, one clear.

"Do you think your dad knows?" I asked Lena.

She shrugged and said, "I guess."

A thing such as a prom was a milestone event so far ahead in our lifetimes we couldn't comprehend it. I didn't think any of us knew the term "endless summer" then, but with finals done, ours had begun.

"Later, gators," Ihaka called with his beaming smile and waved. He scrunched his tall muscular frame into the car. Lena always said she couldn't count the number of girls from school that called the house for him. I wondered which one was his girlfriend.

It had been a long time since he played with us. He still seemed to appear out of nowhere sometimes though, like the time he broke it up when everyone was playing keep away with Dennis Clancy's hat after his chemo treatment and calling him Uncle Kojak. I remember when Tavish was born he said they would form a band and be like Alex and Eddie Van Halen someday. I think the real reason I still liked him was because—even though our relationship had been reduced to mostly friendly waves—he remained a benevolent force in an increasingly hostile world. I thought of him as the big brother I never had.

I waved and listened to the flurry of questions bouncing back and forth.

"He's allowed to drive?"

"Is the prom like a date?"

"You think he's going to *do it* with his girlfriend?"

We watched him drive away then divided into teams, teams we'd probably keep for Ringolevio later.

After kickball and after dinner everyone was back in the street, along with the fireflies rising from the lawns and the songs of the first tree frogs of the season in the warm air. Despite the day seeming like every other day, something felt different, like there was a joke unfolding that I wasn't in on. Chris wasn't his bigmouth self, directing everyone to take places and get set for the game; maybe that was it.

"What's going on, we starting?" I asked Chris.

"Um, yeah, in just a bit. Come on in the back yard, we're starting there."

"What? Base is the telephone pole. We have to start there."

"No, come on, base is at the Thomsons' shed, we're starting there."

"What?"

"Yeah, it is. Come on!"

I followed Chris to the shed. Our whole team followed.

I found Lena and Alice Haninski already there behind the shed. Members of their team appeared behind them, blocking that way out. Something was definitely different and it didn't feel like a joke.

"Hey, come on, we're already hiding here," Lena said. "Go hide in the Rodriguez's yard behind the gate if you want."

"We're not hiding. We're not playing yet," Alice said.

"We're not?" Lena said.

"No," Chris said. "It's Prom day. Two people have to kiss. We can't start the game until two people kiss."

Everyone laughed. Was everyone in on it? I noticed Matt, Alice's little brother wasn't laughing. He slipped out of the crowd and back into the yard.

"That's stupid," I said.

"No, that's the rules," Chris said.

I did not like his serious tone.

"No one wants to do that," I said. "How are we going to decide who?"

"We already have, Jew Boy," Chris said. "We picked you, Jew Boy, and Loch Ness Monster girl."

"Chris, aren't you Jewish too?"

"I am. Doesn't matter. You two are kissing."

"I'm not kissing anyone."

Chris scooted back and wrapped his arm around me in a bear hug. Alice held Lena's arms behind her back.

Most of the time the mess of kids went for easier targets. Ones that didn't snap back. The most common attack I got was how it was unfair that Hanukkah was like eight Christmases. I never told them we were lucky if we could afford chocolate. My usual retort was "Well, it's not fair that half my family got the gas chamber and you have all your cousins and aunts and everyone on Christmas."

"Pick someone else," Lena said.

"We already decided," Alice said.

There was nowhere to run. Both ways out from behind the shed were blocked. I looked at the faces. I knew who the real lowlifes were, like Alice and Chris, and which ones weren't brave enough to stand up to them.

I knew I could break myself free from Chris. And I could get myself over the fence pretty fast, but then what would happen to Lena?

"Guys, this is wrong," I said.

Chris tried to move me to Lena but found he could not. Then he figured they could just push her. As Alice forced Lena closer to me, she started crying.

"Let her go," I demanded.

Lena's father, with Matt at his side, appeared behind Alice and Lena. The mess of kids facing them scrambled. Within seconds it was chaos. Kids hopping the fence into the Siegel's yard. Bumping into each other, deciding which way to run. Mister Thomson was only focused on Lena, though. After determining she was alright, he ordered her to go inside to her mom.

Chris had let go of my arms but didn't run. I wondered if Mister Big Mouth was going to try to play innocent and talk his way out of this.

"Mister Thomson," he said. "We were just playing a game—"

He stopped talking because he could see just like I did that Mister Thomson was ready to blow. Chris bolted and jumped on the fence. Mister Thomson was on him in a flash, pushed him up and flipped him over with a fierceness I'd never seen from him before. I heard Chris land with an awful thump.

"What about the Loch Ness Monster now?" Mister Thomson yelled.

I could hear Chris crying in anguish.

Mister Thomson yelled at him from over the fence. I didn't understand the language. Was it Scottish?

I discerned one word of his outburst.

"*Taniwah.*"

It stuck out to me. I thought it was a curse word. Maybe something he learned from his wife or when he was in New Zealand.

Done yelling at Chris, he turned to me and I thought I was in for it. I was about to run when I realized his rage had turned to tears.

"Why didn't I stop him, Ronnie? It's my fault. Why did I let him?"

In my confusion I thought he was talking about Chris and I tried to explain that nothing had happened. He grabbed me and I shrieked, though his grip immediately softened. He just held me and sobbed. After a minute I wriggled free and left him there, sobbing.

I emerged into the back yard, walked along the side of the house and to the front lawn; to my surprise, everyone was there—all our parents were out in the street. There was a cop car in front of the house. Holy shit, was I in trouble? I didn't do anything. Why was this happening? Then I saw Mrs. Thomson sitting on the front step, crying, flanked by two police officers.

My parents were there on the lawn with everyone. When we met eyes they started crying too. It seemed like everyone was saying Ihaka's name. I thought, "Oh no. What's he done now? He's in some serious trouble," and then I learned he would never be in trouble again. He wouldn't know one day more of this endless summer, or any other. Dressed in a tux, with a flower for his date from his mom's shop and liquor from his dad, he met his end with his drunk jock-ass buddies, trapped in a flaming wreck on his way to the prom.

* * *

Staan Creek District, Belize

Lena takes my hand and in the moonlight coming in through the window over our bed contemplates it, as if she is telling my fortune.

"What'd you see out there? In the water?" I ask.

"You really didn't see?"

She runs the tip of one of her slender fingers up and down my index finger.

"It was nothing," she says.

"Nothing?"

"You saw the lizard?" she says. "The one that ran on the water?"

"The basilisk, yeah."

She moves her finger in a repeating pattern along the back of my hand. It is like she is tracing the path on a map.

"I know what's wrong with you," she says. "I know what's wrong with your life. You like monsters."

She places her finger over her lips, telling me not to speak.

"I want to tell you… I'm a monster too," she says.

In the stillness all the night sounds and lull of the ocean drowns the sound of our breathing.

"One day you'll learn to hate me for it—but not tonight."

I'd forgotten how the feel of softness differs from memory. How a kiss is the one certain way to stop your mind from spinning.

* * *

I wake in the dead of night and she is not next to me. The door is open, letting the night air in. I see her on the beach, trudging through the sand. She moves a few paces then makes a tight turn. Then she walks some more and turns again, as if she's navigating a maze. She must be sleepwalking. I remember hearing that waking a sleepwalker is dangerous so I sit on the doorstep and watch. She doesn't stop till the Southern Cross is in the sky just before dawn. After I am certain she is still, I take her hand and gently guide her back to bed.

* * *

Under the late afternoon sun, I feel like we're acting like the couple she says we are not. Dozing in the beach chairs. Watching the birds at the edge of the water in comfortable silence together.

Lena takes an icy Belikin from our little Styrofoam cooler. I think she's going to offer me one.

"You know. I get it," she says. "He never forgave himself for giving Ihaka the alcohol. He started working later, then worked and worked and worked and then… then, one night he never came home. We never saw him again." I remember how Mister Thomson's absence moved from being speculation grown-ups whispered of at picnic benches and dinner tables in the fog of that summer to just being a given. Ihaka's death. And Mister Thomson being gone. Two terrible, incomprehensible things that just… were.

"I don't know what to say. I can't imagine what he was thinking—"

"That's… just not what you do."

She takes my hand in hers. It's cold from the icy beer. In the distance there is a little island out there in the blue. I hope she is daydreaming pleasant thoughts about it but I know she is not.

Later, when the sun is low in the sky and it is time to think about a meal, I speak.

"Your dad? You want to try again?"

"Mmm hmmm," she says.

So we get ready to go out. In the tiny box of the shower I picture her moving on the beach in the dark and it makes me wonder if there are walls everywhere, all around us, only we cannot see them.

* * *

We arrive at Ihaka's to find Nadine, the gray-haired expat hippie who works for Lena's dad, tending the bar. The stools are empty and there's one other couple having drinks at one of the plastic tables under the trees.

"Mister Thomson here?" I ask.

"Marty's day off," Nadine says. "Maybe he'll be in, though. Maybe he won't."

I thank her and ask her if she's ever been to the condos next door.

"Don't go there," she says.

"Why? Bad parking?"

She gestures for us to lean in.

"Some days just before dawn, when the Southern Cross comes up, you can see the ghosts of all the people who killed themselves and drowned in the cenote."

"Come on," I say. "Don't give us that shit."

"What? You don't believe in ghosts? Okay, you want the truth? I'll tell you. The place was built by a drug dealer…"

"So?"

"Um, so you want to mess around with someone like that?"

"I thought the story was that the drug dealer is dead," Lena says.

Nadine shrugs, apparently out of fodder for the story.

"What you all havin'?"

"Before I order," Lena says. "About… Marty. I saw him on TV. Is it really as awesome working here as it looks?"

"Before I answer. Tell me, is your boyfriend a good tipper?"

"Well, I am, for sure. Two melonballs, please," she says and puts too much cash on the bar top.

"Well, in that case," Nadine says. "Hmmm. Old Marty? Well… he's a good boss but hooo— if you want a good story, be here when he takes out his books and starts talking."

"Talking about what?" Lena asks.

Nadine leans closer again.

"Granted, I've got a lot of explaining to do before I meet my maker," she says. "But only Jesus was meant to walk again after passing through the valley of shadow, know what I mean… "

A sick expression comes over Lena's face.

Mister Thomson emerges from a cluster of big ferns behind the table with the couple. He's carrying a paper box full of green-skinned, spiky guanabanas.

"Lena? I thought that was you, yesterday," he says.

"Dad?"

"I thought I was seeing things. Then you were gone before I could turn around."

He sets the box on the bar, runs the remaining steps to us, and throws his arms around Lena.

"I thought you were gone forever," Lena says, her face buried in his shoulder.

"I thought I was too."

"I love you. I mean… *I hate you.* I can't even… "

"What are you doing here? How—"

"We saw you on television, Mister Thomson."

"Right. I should have figured that."

"Dad this is—"

"Ronnie from next door, hello Ronnie."

"Sir. Mister Thomson. How are you?"

"Wondering what the fuck you're doing in my bar after thirty years? How are *you*? Don't answer that. You're beautiful, darling," he says to Lena. "You can't imagine how much I've missed you."

"Really?"

"Ronnie. Nadine. I'd like some time alone with my daughter. Nadine, after that table we're closed tonight."

"Right," I say. "Lena, you okay?"

"Mmmmm hmmm," she says.

"I'll just… go for a walk then."

"I'll come with," Nadine says. "Follow me."

I follow her past the plastic tables into the jungle. After a minute we come upon a storage shed and the bathroom, which is an outhouse in a small clearing overlooking the beach.

"I know you," she says. "You played drums with… don't tell me—it's on the tip of my tongue."

"Okay, I'm not going to tell you."

She rustles through her shorts pocket and produces a box of Colonials and a lighter.

"Is that really his daughter?"

"Yeah."

"You two a thing?"

"No."

Inside the cigarette box are a dozen hand-rolled joints.

"Wanna wade out into the surf and get high? It's shallow for a thousand yards."

"I'm hitting the head," I say. "Why don't you go and I'll be there in like… ten minutes?"

I have no intention of following. I watch until I see her enter the water and hope she doesn't see me heading in the direction of the condos.

* * *

I arrive at the greenhouse to find the two side doors are open. Inside, most of the mist has dissipated and the table is empty. The thing, whatever it was, is gone.

A slender racoon-like creature is climbing on a tree where the path to the sinkhole begins. It stops its progression towards a twiggy bird nest and regards me. It's focused on my feet. I glance down and see a spider the size of my palm crawling along the soft earth. I hurry along the path, watching where I step.

From a hundred yards away I can see starlight illuminating the sinkhole. Even in the night the water is crystal clear. Tranquil and still. As I near, I notice a large indentation in the ground near the bank where Lena was sitting yesterday. A single wet bandage hangs from the prickly bark of a small palm.

I carefully move to the edge and stare into the water, hoping to see something—a crocodile or anything—in there, but there is only the reflection of the trees and the stars and the stone side disappearing into the depths.

I move along the circumference of the sinkhole, as Lena did yesterday, brushing fronds and branches away from my face, careful not to put my hands on something sharp or on a snake or spider. Maybe a different vantage will give me a clue to what she was thinking. I picture her on the beach, sleepwalking. Then sitting at the bar. What could she and her dad be saying right now? With all the years that have passed, how much remains of the people that they were? Is it the nature of being a family to always hone in on what's still there?

Something moves on the tree in front of me where I am about to place my hand. As I pull it away, I sense motion in my peripheral vision. A snake is wrapped around the young hardwood and the cluster of figs and hanging vines draping the thick gumbo limbo. Only it can't be a snake; the white, scaly coil is as fat as my torso. There's a pink and green shimmer as it inches around the tree. I see motion across the bank. And behind me. The impossibly long white reptilian-fishy body is looped and coiled around the trees of the entire sinkhole.

A crocodile-like head atop a long neck silently emerges from the water, making no ripples. Yellow fins run along its jaws, the same yellow as the single fin of a crest that unfurls on its head. The long neck raises and shifts, moving in line with me. Sentient eyes on either side of its head regard me, like Mister Hieronymus would when the heat light came on in the morning. What kind of fish or reptile is such a jewel-like white color?

I know I am in the dark, yet I find I can see. Or I think what I am doing is seeing. Somehow, I know there are two snakes above me and a bunch of birds sleeping in nests and countless insects at my feet, but I am not seeing them with my eyes. My senses are… confused. Delayed. Mixed up. I can hear all the night sounds but they are muted. I can feel the moist air on my skin and the tree bark I'm gripping, only there's an odd distance like I've taken a step sideways off the planet. The thing's face moves closer. A memory fills me.

There's a ring at my door. It's my ex's kid. Wow—what a difference two years make.

"I know you didn't want me to have it. You said I'd never care for it. I did for a while, but you were right, Ronnie. Please take care of him. I promise I'll never come here again, please don't get me in trouble. I was going to bring it to a pet store but no one wants a grown up lizard when they could have a cute baby."

She didn't wait for me to answer; she put it on my step and ran. When he died, there wasn't anyone for me to call. I wondered what to do with his lifeless body and wondered what would happen—would anyone care—when I finally go?

I watch the white coils slide along the trunks, crossing the space between trees, a living, pulsing circle slithering around the smaller circle of the water hole in the jungle floor.

"What are you?" I say. "Are you lost? I won't tell."

A thought blooms in my mind.

"Are you lost?"

Not words. Not a language. I know as sure as I know when a dog means "I love you" and a cat means "feed me" that the thought belongs to it and that it put it in my mind.

I wonder if I can put *my* thoughts in *its* mind?

"Why did you ask that? Are you just mimicking me? Do you understand me?"

The jar of Mister Hieronymus' hornworms fills my mind's eye. Then the worn-down bar of soap in my shower back home. My empty grocery bags. The fuel meter in my car. In the jeep. The half-empty jug of milk in my fridge. My bank account. My tax forms. My lawn in winter. Spring. Summer. My trees in fall. Lena's house. The Thomsons' shed. A parade of images of mundane things bombards me. All the detritus of the circles and cycles of the things that measure my life. The days. The weeks. The years. The images come and go so fast all is a blur and I can't see.

"*I am leaving here.*"

With that thought the images disappear.

The white coils are gone from the trees. The sinkhole is empty. The sounds of the night have returned to the right places in my ears and in my head. There's a fat bug crawling on my foot. I kick it away. The jungle is starlit dark again and I realize from its absence the thing in the water had radiated a faint light.

The sound of footsteps and breaking twigs reaches me. Something is moving through the brush. I make my way around the bank to where the path meets the sinkhole. Lena's dad is standing there, a black pistol in his hand.

* * *

I feel like I am behind Mister Thomson's shed all over again and he's caught me with Lena. Only this time, things are real. This time I have been kissing her.

"Sir, please," I say. "We're not together."

"My daughter told me, Ronnie. You're lucky I believe her."

* * *

"I wish you hadn't come here, Ronnie," Mister Thomson says and lowers the gun.

"Why are *you* here, sir? You must know the rumors. The ghost story?"

"You know that's all bullshit, Ronnie."

"No suicide? No shoot out?"

Mister Thomson paces and I wish he would say something. I glance into the water. It is clear and motionless. I wonder where Lena is. Is she okay?

"I built this place, Ronnie. Me."

The canals. The houses. The strange bottles and books and greenhouse. All his.

"You built all of this, yet it's empty. Why?

"I have my reasons."

"Because of the sinkhole…"

"You saw it?"

I lie and say I have not.

"Come on, tell the truth, Ronnie. Did the Taniwah… speak to you?"

"Speak to me? No. Um, what are we talking about?"

He paces some more, then sits on the ground; the same spot Lena had chosen. He directs me to sit. I'm nervous about how close our feet are to the edge of the water.

"When I met Lena's mother in New Zealand, I wasn't much older than a boy. In my time, after school you became a soldier or joined the merchant marine. I found myself in a place, a lot like here, near where Lena's mother grew up.

"Something was in the water there."

"It told me I would marry Lena's Mom and we would have three children."

He's fighting tears and getting red in the face. Like he was that day behind the shed when he flipped Chris Eisman over the fence and broke his leg. I'm scared of the gun.

"It never told me the pain I would know. That I would… lose Ihaka. When I told my wife, she had a name for it. But she said such things weren't real, like the thing in Loch Ness."

"Mister Thomson. I never got to tell you. I'm sorry about… Ihaka, about everything."

He produces a thick bundle of cash tied with a band from his back pocket.

"I never thought I'd be gone for good, Ronnie. I know how I let Lena down. I know that now. I just thought… I could just find it again. It would know what to do. It would know how to make things right. Weeks became months. Months became years."

I want to tell him it's never too late. Only I don't know if the words are true. I know the weight of years he speaks of. How time can wear on us—how we still might look like the people we once knew, yet there is really nothing left.

"Ronnie. Ronnie. Ronnie from next door. Belize is beautiful. Such a beautiful place. Here's what you're going to do. You're going to take Lena around. You're going to tell her that her Old Man is just what he appears to be, an old salty bartender who invested his money like the wealthy barber did. Tell me you understand."

"Yes, sir. I got it."

He hands me the cash.

"You're never to come here again. Not to the bar. Not to the complex. Not to this cenote. Don't come back. If you do you won't find me. When you leave me, you will take Lena to breakfast and you will be on your way, do you hear me?"

The name of the restaurant he says is the one the old couple told me about. I stifle my laugh because I realize Martin Thomson is a man used to giving orders. A man comfortable with that gun. Had there ever been a liquor store that he worked at, at all?

I believe everything he's said about Loch Ness and New Zealand and I also know the stories about these condos are true, only he is the criminal. He is the ghost. I know what that feels like, and I hate that his life and what he has done makes a kind of godawful sense to me. I have a million things to ask him, but I don't dare say a single thing other than, "Yes, sir, I will do as you say, sir."

* * *

I put the wad of money on the bed next to our packed bags.

"So that's where he ran off to. To go find… you?" Lena says.

"He wanted you to know your mom never wanted for anything. That her account was always flush, more than flush. He paid for the house, for your school. For everything."

"All these years? She knew?"

"I don't know that. She knew she was taken care of, though."

"All these years and I couldn't find him," she says.

It would be cruel to ask if she knew what she was looking for, or if she even knew how to look at all, so I remain silent.

"Back when we were kids," she says. "Do you think they were pushing us together for a reason?"

I'm careful with what I'm going to say next. There are no reasons. No meanings. Constellations aren't real, they are only the shapes we make of things—

"Oh, don't answer," she says. "Don't worry! I don't think we're soul mates. We're not even a couple."

"Are you lost?"

Why did it ask? Why did it show me the flotsam of my life? It dawns on me after all these years I've never given returning to California a second thought.

"So, all of Belize, huh?" Lena says. "You know where I want to go first?" I want to feel her lips on mine again. I want the quiet of mind. The abandon. The rush it brings—but the charge we felt last night is gone. In its place is an excitement we once knew, a sensation not unlike the juvenile thrill of sneaking out your bedroom window.

I am going to listen to Mister Thomson, and I am going to take her to breakfast and then to wherever she wants, but first I know she wants as much as I do to see the sinkhole one more time before we go.

* * *

The moon is down. The sky is dark. We almost don't realize that Lena's dad is still there, at the edge of the sinkhole, another slender shape among the silhouette of the trees.

I gesture to Lena that we should turn around and go. She refuses. We remain perfectly still in the dark of the tree-covered path. There is nothing left to do but watch him standing there. He must be looking into the water. There's no sign of anything other than lizards and birds and the sounds of their awakening with the coming change to daylight.

Lena's dad shifts and I see he's holding his gun. As he lifts it to his head, I bring my hands over Lena's mouth and eyes.

Thankfully he lays the gun on the ground. I remove my hands from Lena's face, mine all apologies for the forceful way I tried to shield her.

He sits and takes off his shoes. Then unbuttons his shirt. We watch him slide out of his clothing, ease himself from the bank and into the water.

He swims to the center. We watch him submerge. And wait for him to surface. After a minute I wonder how long he can hold his breath. After a few minutes more I wonder if there was any way we could have missed him come up, though I know there is none. He's gone, just like before. As the sky lightens, together we move to the bank and look into that crystal clear water for any sign of him, but find nothing. Just the last traces of the stars before morning.

On Darkened Lawns

IT WAS A DARK SUMMER NIGHT during the big brown out of '05. The trains weren't running and my girlfriend, Kerri, was stuck in the city. Even so, with no power to the traffic lights I was staying off the roads, so I won't be going to see her tonight. Putting off the inevitable. On my way to Callahan's to drown my sorrows, I noticed my neighbor's lawn jockey was missing from its place among the parade of lawn deer, lawn ducks, and ceramic mushrooms that blighted an otherwise pleasant green-grassed, well-manicured, shrubbed, suburban front yard.

My relationship with Kerri was on borrowed time. Something about the old men at Callahan's and the bartender, who looked like she could have been something once, comforted me as I struggled with the question of "what does one do with the good times once a relationship is gone."

I drank myself into quite a stupor and after midnight. I figured it was time to shamble home before I risked not waking up tomorrow. I walked home, no closer to any answers. Still lost in thought, I wondered why my keys didn't work in my door. I looked at the lawn and realized I must have turned down the wrong block.

It was full of lawn jockeys, their lanterns shining with the glow of thousands of fireflies.

I stood there thinking, *damn, some kids really did a good one.* And then I saw the jockeys were moving—escorting kids to and from the corner where the bus stops; trailing men in suits with brief cases to their cars. Everywhere, scenes of suburban life were being played out like ghostly recorded images and the lawn jockeys followed, illuminating them with their yellow-green, too-bright lantern light.

And for a second it all made sense, I understood the place of these purposeless lawn ornaments in the universe. Then I reminded myself of the hour and the impossibility of it all and told myself that it couldn't be.

"No, you had it right the first time," said a blue and white jockey standing next to me. "This makes perfect sense. You've traveled far to see us, my friend."

As he spoke I had a vague recollection of passing out. Was that my body face down on the steps there behind the little cast iron man?

"So where do you want to go?" he said.

"To see Kerri, I guess," I said without thinking. It came out naturally.

The clunk of horseshoes on asphalt filled the night. The jockey smiled and now that I heard the echoing sound I realized the rest of the commotion was strangely noiseless.

"Your question," the jockey said. "Good times. They are a noble pursuit in and of themselves. They are never destroyed, even when you and she are no more."

A pair of tall, strong horses, the same yellow-green as the lantern light, galloped down the block and stopped in front of the house. I remembered tripping. Stumbling. Falling on the brick stairs. My head smashing on the concrete.

"So, I'm not going to make it to work tomorrow after all, am I?" I asked.

The jockey's fixed expression seemed somber as he stiffly shook his head from side to side. Then he climbed on one of the horses.

"Come on," he said. "Kerri awaits. I shall race you there."

In Search of Elephant Corners

THE THIEF'S SHADE WAS trying to follow Sylvie back to Elephant Corners. Again. She heard the phantom whine of her motorbike's engine though it was nowhere to be seen on the street crowded with the bustle of day sellers closing shop and patrons gathering for the night market. She'd been studying under the elder fortunetellers for weeks. The half-day search on her motorbike to find the four elephant shaped buildings she called home seemed so far away.

"Why did it take me so long to find my way here?" Sylvie had asked, before her daily walk to the market to fetch fresh chicken bones for the divination cups. "We are almost in the center of the city, right in plain sight. For anyone to see or follow."

"Ganesha is the remover of obstacles," the fortune woman called Katerina had answered, then affectionately patted an elephant figurine that looked much like the sculpted face of the building.

Had it been Ganesha who removed the obstacles preventing her from finding the Fortune Tellers? Ganesha who guided the thief who stole her motorbike? It wasn't Ganesha following her now. She could feel the thief's yearning. Not just for her. To find Elephant Corners.

The accident that had claimed him had been meant for her. It involved a blown tire. A refugee from the city of Phiros, an old hero of the Origami circuit. Chickens. A lot of them. And a contraband shipment of vampire vine.

The shade followed her most evenings. And was always thwarted by one fortuitous distraction or another. One time by a raucous trip of escaped chickens. Another by a pretty lady muttering charms under her lacy veil. Yet another by a tiny rainstorm moving almost purposefully through the stairway alleys.

But today was the day of dragon-kites and tombstones (at least according to the calendar of Sylvie's ancestral home), the day spirits will rise and walk in flesh of the unwary if given a chance.

The shade slowly but steadily pursued her through the market streets and winding alleys. To Sylvie's dismay no distractions appeared to hinder it.

Sylvie ducked into a side street hoping to lose it with speed but the egress was blocked by an ostrich caravan. She gulped, trying to gather the courage to run back out and past the invisible, menacing presence. The sputter-pop of her lost motorbike was almost upon her.

"Just go away," she cried, afraid the shade would touch her and ride her body back to Elephant Corners.

The motorbike sounds retreated. The shade had moved to a piece of glow-taffy on the cobblestones. Sylvie spied another piece at the entrance to the next alley. A trail? She was in luck—the shade followed and Sylvie ran home.

"Why," Sylvie asked Katerina once she was safely behind the door-leg of the blue elephant. "How did I escape? Why can no one find Elephant Corners when it is in plain sight?"

"Ganesha protects this place," she answered. "Today you learned he is also the placer of proper obstacles."

Sylvie thought about it. The shade had wanted something. From her. From Elephant Corners. The fortune tellers must have had a reason to prevent her death in the bike crash.

Maybe if she continued her studies she'd be able to find the answer in patterns of the past or divine its shape from the ripples it sent into the ever changing future.

Human Impersonation Day

HUMAN IMPERSONATION DAY comes once a year. My sister and I have our pockets full of shiny things and are trying to get to the rooftop unnoticed. Last year, I made it backstage for the Van Halen concert at Nassau Coliseum and placed green candies in all the dressing rooms. She went to the Museum of Knives in the Catskills and left quizzical poems on strips of black paper for the staff to find. That day she broke the rules of reverse-thieving though, and absconded with one of their blades.

* * *

Outside the windows the New York City skyline pretends to be permanent; its reflection shimmering in the Hudson. The humans here are costumed and dancing. We'll have to weave through them to get to the stairs.

"Look, that one is dressed as Edgar Allen Poe," my sister whispers.

"Poe," I say.

It comes out almost like a human word.

My sister's disappointed look shows concern I might blow our secret. That we are more than we seem. She doesn't know I have a secret too.

I didn't tell her the truth when I agreed to join her mission.

* * *

"Ooh, great costume. What are you?"

Instead of answering, I give the human guarding the stairs a chocolate coin, a paper flower, and a squid made of sparkling gold sludge from my pocket.

"Hmmmn. Still can't let you pass. The King of the Rooftop is up there tonight."

I know.

I produce more Chanukah gelt. A bottle cap. A polished dime. A priceless, ancient silver coin. A steel screw from the glasses you lost last summer.

My sister shakes her head condescendingly, then takes the man's hands in hers, looks into his mind and gives him glimpse of the void between worlds. His blue left eye widens. I want to poke it out and eat it.

Then we are ascending in the inelegant manner of non-winged-things.

* * *

A peacock my sister once knew is parading on the line where the rooftop crosses into dreams. Things that look like child's impersonation of birds dance with humans on a mosaicked floor. The tiles depict spirits eating birds, birds eating spirits, all of them entwined with the serpents from the King of the Rooftop's head. I thought we'd have to get him alone. The spinning humans don't notice our approach. Their dance mirrors their lives outside the rooftop. Those lives a mirror of the solar system. Of the universe. Of everything. My sister puts poems in the

King's pockets. Songs in his mind. Soft pecks on his face.

I study it. It pleases me. I think I will take it.

* * *

"Give me your knife."

"Why?"

"I'm not changing back."

"That's not the way this works."

I love my sister despite her penchant for rules she thinks will stave off meaninglessness.

I reveal my secret in my question.

"Sister, will you visit me next year, on Human Impersonation Day, when I am king of this rooftop?"

The peacock chortles in approval of what is about to come.

Phantom Constellations

Anza-Borrego Desert, California. 1992.

"ONCE YOU VISIT THE DESERT you never look at the sky the same again, no matter where you are," Chase says to me. "You'll see."

"I believe you."

And I do. After the bluff ahead the world is nothing but unblemished, powder-blue.

In the rear-view I watch her attempt to pass her cigarette to Harrison. She's so high she misses that his attention is captured by the almost-dusk-time shadows of all the cactus and brush on the sand and winding road. Her not-dyed blond hair and light eyes come from her mother's side. Her Mom met her Dad when she was stationed over in Miramar, she told us last night over rolled tacos in the joint across from the Photo-mat where she works. Her height's from her mother too, she said. Skin color and distinct nose from her Dad. Along with the knowledge of all the things that make Southern California Southern California—the beach, the desert, the food, the drugs.

"You have to try the tamales Dad brings up from his abuela in Mexico," she told Harrison, who wasn't enamored with the "taco-sticks," at all. She taps his leg insistently, causing the cigarette head to fall. Neither notice. Har's framing the endless open-space and sky moping that he's out of film, I can tell. I wonder if he's going to start in on that how-nothing-ever-goes-right-for-him business again. Maybe he'll recognize that finding Chase was something going right for him, above and beyond the free film. She says she loves him. If she doesn't really see him, does she even really know him though?

Moon's trying to open the passenger window. The child lock has her stymied—her inept fumbling the opposite of my first glimpse of her last night back at Chase's place. I didn't believe my eyes—thought I was looking at Chase standing in the doorway, silently watching me, though I'd just watched her lustily "retire" to her room with Har. Was this Chase's twin? So the same in so many ways except for the glaring opposites of Moon's dark hair and alabaster skin.

"Oh, okay, we're here. Stop here, stop here," Chase says.

Beyond the metal rail separating the pavement from the unfathomable drop, the view is unimpeded for miles and miles and miles. Myriad nuances of color and every shade of brown and white and gray. Winding roads snake through border towns to the edge of the wild spaces; everything washed out and hazy from the heavy sun almost ready to set—the lone shape burning in the perfect sky.

The plan is to watch it here before heading off down into that view to have a campfire dinner and night under the stars.

Moon's figured out the window and has it open before I have the truck stopped in the parking spot. A blast of hot air sends the chemical note of her sunscreen along with the aroma of sage and brush and ozone at me. I cut the engine. Without the AC blowing we realize we are surrounded by… stillness. All four of us are taking it in. The motion of birds on the scrub and the gentle breeze doesn't break the sensation. Moon adjusts her light blue half-shirt and white terry cloth shorts and slides herself halfway out the window. I gently touch her leg and tell her to be careful. She responds with a flirtatious wriggle of her hips.

"Its amazing out here," she says. She makes eye contact with me in the side mirror, sticks out her tongue and taps the tip twice with her slender, manicured index finger. "You want to? You really should join us."

Her silver-sparkle-polished nail catches the sun.

"I'm good," I say. "Still good. Still the one driving."

Sixty-eight days sober and counting is better than good. Taking care of myself. I agreed to this jaunt because I'm taking care of them. I eye the white gift-bow I've left on the rear view. I'm done letting people down. Every day since I've been out has been work and studying. Switching the NY plates for California is the final thing left.

"Holy shit, look! Look at that!" Chase says.

Moon twists herself to see. Harrison is up against the window.

"What the hell," he says.

The occupants of the two other cars are out and at the rail gawking at a long white line of a cloud that has just appeared out of nowhere in the sky. The first thing I think is that's one of those ropy, high-the-hell-up-there clouds. But aren't they always in big groups? This one is hanging low right in front of the sun.

I watch the line… bending. And… inflating. In seconds it's become a bow arcing over the valley.

We pour out of my truck into air alive with kinetic certainty.

The bow folds over and over and becomes a puffy mass. A storm cloud? A giant undulating herald of desert rain? Whatever it is, it's forming and reforming its contour with the impossible speed of a time-lapse photo; glowing oranges and pinks and reds, all the setting sun's colors, emanating from it. Brighter than any fireworks. It's all so surreal because the angles don't seem right for the reflection or projection or whatever the hell I am looking at.

"Hell of a thunderhead," one of the other onlookers says.

"Ha. No thunderhead, look at the sky. Folks over at the air force base are laughing their asses off right now."

I hear the words but there is only this feeling of… stillness. There is only the feeling of… desert air alive with a coming storm? There is only a wave of… comfort… my bones telling me everything is all right. There is only the shape… that is no shape… that is the cloud.

"I want to stay this way," Chase says. "I want to live this way, right?"

Before I can decide if she has made a statement or asked a question, I laugh in recognition that I know exactly what she means.

Across the lot I hear the word "right" spoken by the other people.

Moon hands me a boxy disposable camera, one of the green panorama ones from the supermarkets. "Take a picture of me. Get it all."

The cloud is a convex half-sphere. A wave. A giant tidal wave rolling towards the bluff.

Moon poses, slightly lifting one long leg and holding her back-length hair in a messy bun. Chase and Harrison are staring into the sky, standing alarmingly still.

There is nothing wrong here, I tell myself. There is only beauty. Beneath the feeling of peace, part of me is screaming. I'm the life guard. I'm the adult here today. Fuck this.

I manage to wrangle all three of them back inside the truck. I hit the button to send up the windows and crank the air. I fumble my keys into the ignition and that's when Harrison pushes his door open, beelines to the guard rail, and climbs.

* * *

Harrison has put the rolls of black and white film up front and is scouring the Photo-mat's aisles for a frame Nehru's tasked him to procure as a prop for his shoot.

"Do you believe in love at first sight," the counter-girl says to me absently as she watches Har shop.

On her name tag "Chase" is hand-written over "Chelsea."

I'm in my blue work clothes. My name's embroidered on my chest. Came straight from my shift to some bar on the Pacific Beach strip to meet Har who came to see me. First time since I got out. When they gave me my stuff back with it there was a letter he'd sent to Mom and Dad's back home. He'd scored a real job. A good one as an assistant to a director on a real Hollywood movie they are shooting nearby in Ocean Beach.

Har comes to the counter with a frame and actually introduces himself in a rare display of extraverted-ness and boyish charisma.

"How much?"

"It's yours," Chase says.

"Really? Is this because I'm the only one here without a name tag?"

"For you doll, yeah really. Anything. Take it. And take the film."

"Whoa. Guess this means I'm gonna have to keep the dough Nehru gave me."

"Who?"

"My boss. Nehru Casteltinni." he says.

I wince at how pretentious he sounds. Chase remains starry-eyed.

"I'm about to close up. Want to go for tacos? You can use the dough for that. Cool?"

"I've never had," Har says.

"What? You've never had Mexican food?"

"We're sort of newcomers. From New York," I say.

Chase locks up the place. We're close enough to the beach to smell the ocean on the night air. Har steps into the street.

"Hey, you can't do that, that's jaywalking," Chase says.

She leads us to the corner where we cross the four-lane road then double back to the taco joint. Har disapproves of this route but remains quiet. He must like Chase. I hope he doesn't go off on how unfair he thinks he's being treated by Nehru.

I notice we're the only white guys as soon as we're through the door. Chase and Har are rambling on like they've known each other forever, oblivious to the glances from disapproving faces.

We sit at a linoleum-topped table. Chase orders and within minutes three iced teas and three plates of fried rolled tacos topped with loads of guac are in front of us.

"Why does this iced tea taste like … fruit?" Har asks.

"This is California, baby," Chase says.

Har pushes guacamole around with a fork and I realize what a big baby he is and wonder why people ever fall into his orbit.

"Taco-sticks" and iced tea is a bust so, food unfinished, we load into my truck, both of them hopping into the back seat. Chase directs me down the Five to Chinatown, to please Har.

"San Diego's so clean and tiny compared to New York," I say. "And no traffic."

Neither reply. They're kissing. I interrupt with a cough when we hit the city.

"This is Chinatown?" Har says.

"Well, Old Town is more picturesque," Chase says.

"What's Old Town?"

"All Mexican food," I say. "You wouldn't like it."

The entrance to the Chinese place is flanked by two dragon statues covered in aging golden paint. Inside is dimly lit and inviting. We dine on Kung Pao chicken and black tea, real tea, to Har's liking beneath a ceiling mural of an inky blue sky crowded with stylized old-fashioned golden stars. Chase clicks her worn chopsticks together, wooden ones, not disposables.

"Oh, how many stories those chopsticks can tell," I say.

"See," Har says. "My buddy here's a poet. You can't teach that."

"Oh, so you're in film too?"

"No, I'm a plumber. On my way to being a master plumber. I'm studying for the exam to go to school to get my MBA too."

"He's being humble," Har says. "Only reason he isn't a film maker because he's too busy being the real deal. Life. He's living it for real."

"Wow, who knew? Two New York guys here in California," Chase says.

"Why'd you come out, Harrison?"

There's a pause and I can feel Har's gears spinning, thinking about back home.

"I came here for rehab, not college," I say, so Har doesn't have to answer. "It was my ticket away from brutal New York. I'm an addict. The place got me into a trade, so I stayed."

I think hearing my naked truth out loud puts a scare in Har. Up until six weeks ago he was living in his Mom's basement among impossible clutter. His screenplays and story boards and VHS tapes stacked among the detritus of his broken family living above, all the broken things not thrown away, only accumulating—poison anchors adding weight to lives already sinking, sinking, sunk. Just thinking about the numb silences and wrenching screaming matches and worse has my stomach unhappy.

"I'm a nomad," Har says.

With a glance he instructs me not to counter him with the truth.

"I'm really actually a vagabond. A traveling bartender—but I took this job shooting this film."

"Right, your film."

"Well, it's a Nehru Casteltinni film. Ya know, my boss, so it's kinda his film but he's all coked-up and partied-out, so I'm setting most of the shots and doing all of the leg work. I'm sure the producers are going to credit me. I didn't even think the fiend was going to give us this time off for Thanksgiving week. So hey, my first time in San Diego, first chance I had to visit my man here."

He pats me on the back. For a second I believe him, that he's okay, living out our childhood dreams of making movies. And that he's going to ride into the sunset for the both of us.

"Oh, you have to come to the desert, then, if this is your first time here! We all have to go. Let's do it! My Dad used to always take us Thanksgiving time."

After dinner we wind up back at her place, a little low-rise, cute but in disrepair, in a cluster of similar low-rises a couple of blocks from the beach, back in Pacific Beach near the Photo-mat. The main room we enter into has a surprisingly stuffed book case, a coffee table with a full ash tray, and a TV hooked up to Sega. I don't see a couch but there are lots of big pillows.

Chase takes Har by the arm and leads him to a door to the right of the kitchen area, which comprises the far wall opposite the entrance.

"We're going to retire and get to know each other better, she says. "You gonna crash here?"

They don't wait for me to answer.

I go to the bookcase and decide what I'm gonna do. It's full of astrology books, self-help stuff, new age titles, and a ton of fantasy paperbacks. I pick up a bottle of fancy-looking perfume from among the stacks.

As I smell the cap, I realize someone's watching me. I turn and see a woman in a black silk robe with long black hair and pale skin leaning in the doorway opposite the one Chase and Har disappeared into. For a second I think I'm looking at Chase. A dark-haired, ethereal, poised and confident Chase. We stare at each other silently.

"Hey boss," the woman finally says, then shuffles to the fridge.

There's a big yellow sun on the back of her robe. And from something about the way she closes the distance I can tell she's using. There's a sound from her room. Someone's in there with her.

"Smells better on my skin," she says.

Everything about her—every motion, the way her gaze lingers, is saying, "Do you want to join us?" Maybe it's just me—projecting. Maybe it's just my mind playing tricks on me.

Joining her would be oblivion. Joining her would be to taste the sweetness of nothingness. The sweetness of lost time. Cool heat eclipsing my mind's questions. Will I pass the exam? Will I make master plumber? Will I get into the union? Will I ever start my own shop? How long until I take over the insurance payments on the truck to show my folks I'm not a waste?

"I said it smells better on my skin. I never understand why boys like video games so much."

She's still speaking as she returns to the darkness of her room. I distract myself by looking away and recounting multiple choice questions in my head. I don't glance over even after I hear the door close.

* * *

Sometime in the night I'm woken by someone walking past me. I've passed out on the pillows. An older woman in a black pencil skirt is buttoning her white business shirt on the way out the door. I drift back to sleep.

I wake again after what feels like only minutes to someone kicking my side. A different woman is standing there. *California is the land of beautiful women* is the first thought my sleeping self manages.

"I warned you already," she says in a thick Russian accent. "No staying the night. Now I'm going to have to shoot you in the face."

My eyes are blurry but I think she's holding a gun.

"Um, I'm Chase's friend. I've never been here before."

She is holding a gun. And a lit cigarette in her other hand.

"Seriously. My friend is in there with Chase now. We met at the Photomat."

"Oh, you have New York accent. And that is your New York truck?"

"Yes, yes."

This seems to satisfy her.

"All you American boys look the same."

She takes another disdainful look at me. Then trudges to the fridge for a beer and disappears into Moon's room.

* * *

In the morning all is chipper and cheer and sunshine. I don't see a reason to mention my nighttime encounters. Whoever they were, they're gone, and Chase and Moon are a flurry of cigarettes and coffee and scrambled eggs. Chase calls Har "honey" and "dear" and "my film maker." Moon calls me "boss."

"We've been up early, loaded your truck with supplies," Har says. His smiles seem for real. We're going to the desert. He feels like my dear old friend again. The guy from the block I grew up dreaming with. It's been so long since I knew what it felt like to do something just for the hell of it.

* * *

Not far outside of San Diego all the small towns and windmills and aqueducts have me realizing that these West Coast cites really are built on desert.

Peter Gabriel's song "San Jacinto" is on the radio. Three fighter jets in formation soar across the sky perpendicular to the road. Chase says this is quite a common sight. And adds, "Mexico's like ten miles, that way. My Dad knows the routes the drug planes fly, low and close to the mountains to avoid radar."

"Oh yeah, can't *wait* to meet your Dad," Har says.

Chase punches him playfully.

The back seat is their honeymoon palace and they have the clichéd glow of those who have just slept together for the first time. At least Chase does. I see hints of the stress of the shoot on Har's face. In a day or two he'll be back to it. And I can tell his plum job isn't as plum as he's making it out to be. I want to help.

"So, I was wondering if you are going to ask about your contract," I say gently.

"That's not how it works," Har snaps.

The radio fades in and out in a pattern that sounds like morse-code.

"Well, I think that's how it works," Moon says to me, softly. "You're a good friend for telling him."

"I don't want to upset him."

There is an uneasy silence as we roll past the last buildings of some small town and are again flanked by desolate scrublands.

"Without rules. Without boundaries, I'm just a whore," she says.

"I can hear you back here," Har says.

"Then you hear me talking about myself," she replies. "I'm not a prostitute. I'm an escort. The difference is I choose. I choose *who*. I choose *what* I do. Or if I do anything at all. You choose who *you* want to be, Okay?"

I'm worried Har is going to pop. And what am I doing? In a car with a girl we met at the Photo-mat and her escort roommate who uses. Would Har kill me if I came up with some excuse to call this all off?

"Nehru does treat me like his little whore," Har says calmly.

I hear all the hurt he's felt in his entire life in each of his words. I know he's grateful that I'm not turning around, he knows I'm thinking about it.

"Okay," Chase says. "Two more miles or next town, whichever comes first, and no more talking business, okay? Hey, Moon. You ready?"

Moon takes out a square of white paper perforated into tabs from her tiny purse. There are dozens of little yellow suns printed on it. She and Chase open their mouths wide and say "ahhh" through their giggles. Moon tears off two tabs. They each place one of the tabs on each other's tongue.

"You with us?" Chase says to Har.

"Nah, I'm good," he says and laughs.

I recognize this laugh. It says *oh look what craziness we have got ourselves into* and is a further check to make sure I'm not going to rain on his parade.

"The desert is the best," Chase says to me. "I love it there it even when straight. This way it is so much better though. First time in the desert I think you guys should."

"You in?" Moon says.

The last time I ever used I didn't OD, I took a bad needle—who knows what was in it. I was feeling cold and numb and managed to call my Dad before flopping down into a tub of running water to try to warm up. Mom and Dad standing over me, fishing me out was the last thing I remembered before the emergency room where they restarted my heart.

"I'm taking care of him," is all I manage to say.

"Thought so," she says and rolls down the window. She slips her sneakers off and joyously sticks her legs out the window into the wind.

* * *

Har climbs over the guard rail onto the rocky outcrop before the drop as the cloud rolls over him and then us.

For a minute all is smoke. Like inside a plane breaking the cloud layer. Then it is gone. Impossibly fast. We open the doors and check the sky all around. The valley. The mountain pass we came from. Nothing. Just the sunset's last rays dying in a perfectly clear sky.

One of the onlookers is having a smoke. The thick wisps strike me as obscene. We run to the guard rail. Har is perched on the crumbly ledge, clutching his knees, with nothing separating him from the drop. We help him over the rail. He's crying.

"You okay—"

"Give me all the drugs," he says.

"Right on," Moon says and opens her little purse.

"Come on, no," I say.

"Yes. All of it," Har says.

I snatch the square of paper from Moon.

"Careful how you touch that," she says with a giggle.

Har snatches it, rips off a corner and stuffs it in his mouth before I grab it back and return it to Moon.

"Did you see that shit," he says.

"Welcome to California, baby," Chase says and the girls laugh.

Great—now I'm babysitting three people.

We head down the mountain into the desert; there's nothing else to do.

* * *

Chase and Moon are hyperfocused on all the boulders and cactus we pass as we descend. A coyote that darts across the road changes their giggles to a round of intense whispers. Har is telling us in great detail and in one long, long never-ending sentence how he's going to make breakfast for dinner over the fire. I can't stop thinking about the cloud. Is this the way people deal with... happenings like this, or is it just the drugs?

We roll past a rectangular bank of showers and restrooms into the empty campsite. Who wants to be outside in the cold for Thanksgiving? With the sun gone it is hard to believe the day's heat was ever with us.

There're spaces delineated for dozens of cars, each with a roof-sheltered picnic table and fire pit. With no other buildings, no lights except the stars, the landscape is a sprawling city of cactus and rock etched into the warm, glowing sky.

I'm impressed that Har and Chase loaded my truck with an iron pan and eggs and pancake mix. Along with water, and firewood, and two tents.

No sleeping bags, though.

Breakfast for dinner is a masterstroke. And then, without cleaning up, Har and Chase disappear into their tent they've set up in their own camp spot a few spaces away.

Moon and I clean up and set up our tent next to my truck in a spot with a view looking out on the starlit silhouettes of desert plants against the rocky hills ringing the camp site. Inside and zipped up it is still cold; we have no jackets or long pants. I retrieve the wool Mexican-weaved beach blanket I keep my truck and we huddle under it.

Moon rolls over and faces me. I'm very aware of the softness of her skin touching mine. Her leg gently draped on me. Her shallow, steady breath.

"This is nice," she says. "My girlfriend doesn't kiss me anymore."

"Russian girl? Carries a gun."

"Yeah—"

"Met her in the middle of the night. She threatened to shoot me in the face."

"Oh. She's like that. Possession is part of love. Isn't it? The last part to let go…"

"You're letting go? She won't let go?"

"I don't know. Sometimes when things are over and you're still holding on the only things left to grasp are the shadows. You know you could really do good as a plumber. I could run the books. I have these great business suits."

She presses tighter to me. It is good to be warm. To be held. I like that her face—her lips—are so close to mine. It isn't that I don't want to kiss her. A kiss is never just a kiss. With it comes all of her. And all the reasons the addictions have her. Someday I'll be alone and look back at this moment with regret I tell myself as I roll out from under the blanket.

"Long day. I'm hitting the shower."

"Watch out for rattlesnakes," she says.

I retrieve the roll of quarters from the glove box in my truck and cross the empty campsite.

I have enough coins for little packets of soap and shampoo and leave my clothes by the vending machine in the vestibule. I put the rest of my quarters in the box next to the faucets; warm water cascades onto my sand and grime and dried-sweat-coated skin. There are droplets of white light glistening in the rivulets. I look up to see if this is something to do with the light fixture.

Someone's in the vestibule with me. Moon. Standing in the doorway, like last night. Only naked. Her hair is tied up.

"Can I join you? Save water and all? I brought towels, from Chase's bag, ha."

I was hoping she'd fall asleep. I try not to look at her.

"I guess," I say. "Just a shower though, please."

She steps into the water. I watch the drops of white light glisten where the water rolls off her shoulders. She keeps her promise; she showers then exits.

I stay in until my water runs out. I'm grateful for the towel she's left. I get mostly dry and go for my clothes. They're gone.

"Up here," Moon calls.

She's on the building's flat roof.

"Don't worry, it's an easy climb."

It is an easy climb and I hope Chase and Har don't pick this moment to come out of their tent and see me naked.

On the roof, Moon's laying on her back, naked on top of her clothes, staring at the stars. My clothes are laid out next to her. I follow suit and lay down on top of them.

There's something different about the sky. The stars are brighter than I remember. I can see them… glistening. I can see lines of white light coming from them and moving through the sky. Some of the lines reach the desert. And end where they reach pairs of animal eyes in the night. I become aware of the presence of dozens of coyotes near us. Moon has been talking…

"…when you run away you become someone else. Unless you're being chased, then you're running for your life, right? If you are running like that you are still you, you aren't who someone else says you are…"

Is that what I've been doing in California, running? What about Har? Are we brand new versions of us? Have we been chasing ourselves?

"…I don't normally tell people I want to kiss them, but you are going to be famous. A movie star. Maybe a film producer…"

"Did Chase tell you I'm in film?"

"No, I see it in the stars."

"What. How?"

"See that?"

She points to a star. When I nod that I see it, she directs my gaze to six others.

"That's Pleiades. The Seven Sisters."

I realize there are also stars in the black where I previously thought there were none. The faintest points of light. Along with dots all the colors of the spectrum.

"One for each world," she says.

"There are seven worlds? Which world are we in now?"

"I could tell you. It would take all night though. Would you believe me?"

"I don't know what you're going to say. How do I know if I'll believe you?"

"I've seen it so many times before," she says. "People like to stay put. They don't believe even what they see with their own eyes and convince themselves all experiences fit into something safe and known. It's easier that way."

"Like that thunderhead?"

"Is that what you're telling yourself it was?"

"I guess so, I didn't think about it? What was it?"

"I don't know. That's the thing," she says.

I'm distracted by her flat stomach, the curve of her hip, and her pelvis bone. I do not like that I am losing my resolve so I gather my clothes. Chase is singing in the shower below.

"I refuse to make believe and make up meanings," Moon says as I am getting dressed. "That's why the world is so hard for me to live in."

I climb down as Har is walking out of the showers. He's heading away from the campsite and into the desert. I call to him to wait up.

"You two stargazing up there?"

"Something like that," I say. "Did you know there are seven worlds?

"Of course," he says. "Wait, you just said seven seas, right?"

"No, seven worlds."

"Who told you that?"

"Moon," I say.

"Ah, Moon. And you believe her?"

"She said she saw it in the stars, the Pleiades. Its astrology and stuff. It makes sense. I mean it did a minute ago."

"Constellations aren't real," he says. "They're something we make up from what we want to see. The only connections out there are the ones we give and that's just not real. When tonight is over and by that I mean after we shake it off and sleep it off, we got our lives to get back to."

"Where are you going?"

"Right now, I'm high as can be and I'm going to enjoy it on a walk alone in the desert."

He walks a few paces. Then stops and back tracks to me.

"One thing. When the shoot is done and I'm back in LA will you take care of her, please?"

I try to remember him being close to anyone, any woman, any of the girls who've circled him. I cannot. Once he rescued a kitten from a dumpster and even that didn't end well.

"Anything for you, man," I say.

I feel a long way from home as he walks into the night. This is what being grown up must be. Feeling alone and overwhelmed and hoping you've got enough to make it through.

I lay down next to the smoldering fire. The hard earth feels good on my back and I take in the wood smoke on the clean air. I hear Chase in the shower. I know Har is out there in the desert. And I haven't seen Moon come down from her star gazing perch. It dawns on me to build the fire up again. No matter what Har says, I know the four of us form a shape. I know this is not a made-up thing because when I close my eyes, I feel us— four points in the night. Feeling it means it's real, I decide, as I pass into the world of sleep.

* * *

The sun is coming up over the hills, the rock alive with color where the new light touches. A quail darts past, its spiral head feather bobbing. I decide I'm going to sweat last night off and go for a run.

Har, Chase and Moon wake hours later, at the crack of noon. On the drive back to San Diego they remain burnt out. Beneath the energy I have mustered I feel the drag too. I dodged a bullet. Yesterday could have been a real mess. I'm gonna get them back safe then have myself a light dinner and hit the books.

Chase's place looks shabby and sad in daylight. A bunch of sketchy guys are standing around, eyeing my truck as I help everyone carry their stuff inside. I can tell whatever substance I want can be had from them in a heartbeat.

I write my number and address on Har's hand in marker and tell him to call me later. He doesn't.

* * *

The next morning I'm studying on my balcony, hoping Har's going to call before he goes back to work, and realize I should have taken Chase's number.

In the parking area two stories below I see a little sunburst-yellow Miata pull into a spot. Moon's behind the wheel. She does a line on her dashboard then gets out and heads to the stairs. Did Har tell her where I live?

A minute later my doorbell rings. It takes me only a second to decide I'm not going to answer. She knocks on the door. Has she noticed my truck is here? Probably?

The old me would do just one line with her and not care what came next. I come inside and peer through the curtains as she returns to her car and drives away.

Twenty minutes later my phone rings. It's Har. He tells me to meet him and Chase for happy hour at a bar called Jerry's Ice House on the strip at PB.

"Oh, you're a local now?"

"Shut up," he says. "My last night out before going back to work. I'm bartending."

Showboating is more like it.

When I leave my place, outside my door is the disposable camera and a pile of manilla envelopes, from Moon. Full of scripts and stories and movie ideas.

As I drive, I try to wrap my mind around her. She also writes stories? No matter who she is or what her skills are, a girl with a habit is going to do me in. After tonight, keeping myself together is my full-time job again.

Pacific Beach's concrete boardwalk is a California dream. Cyclists, rollerbladers, girls without drug habits are everywhere. Someday, when I have my shit together, I'm going to find one, for me. The wide path runs south to Mission Beach. Does it reach Ocean Beach beyond where Nehru is shooting? I prefer its surfer vibes and sleepy pace to all this flash and color and thumping music. I think of the wood boardwalk back home at Jones Beach.

The big front windows to Jerry's Ice House have been removed and I can see inside to the far wall: dozens of mixed drink machines are lined up side by side, washing machine looking things displaying sugary iced alcohol in bright neon colors, spinning and turning and churning. Young women in tube tops and tight shorts roam the cavernous space with trays of shots in test tubes. I haven't even stepped inside and I hate it already. I tell myself I'm going to stay, for Har.

I find Chase sitting at a tall table a few feet from the bar where Har is stationed. I can hear Har making platitudes about his special cocktails. They don't even serve cocktails here; he's serving ices from those machines. I don't think I've ever had a real cocktail. Maybe a sip at a Chinese restaurant once. Har rambles on about Russian things. Russian drinks. How Nehru's film is somehow connected to something he finds tragically hip about Russia.

The first time I saw him showboating like this, I thought he was desperate for the adoration. It didn't take long for me to realize he was desperate just to be seen—to escape from living in his basement like another discarded thing. It's clear as the sky on the ridge where we saw the cloud that Chase adores him, not because of, but despite all this.

"Having fun?" Chase asks me.

"I'm here for Har," I say. "What do you think? Can we convince him to give rolled tacos another try after this?"

As she answers my eye is drawn to a woman beelining towards Har at the bar. I can't be sure but I think it is Moon's girlfriend. Har is laughing and produces a bottle of vodka and some shot glasses; it looks like they're having fun. Har's smile sours. The woman grabs the vodka bottle and belts him across the face with it. Har folds facedown onto the bar. She hits him over the head, breaking the bottle with a spray of blood and vodka. She runs. I scramble over to Har. Blood is pouring from his head. The left of his face is torn up. I don't see his eye, only the bloody socket.

* * *

I call Har's Mom from the bank of phones in hospital waiting area. No one cares. I sit in the booth, reflecting on how I know the number by heart, the same number it was on all the calls I made growing up. I'm not ready to go back in to see him, so I call my parents.

My Mom goes on about the snow they've been having and then implores me to come home and take a job back home. Dad is stoic about it all and tells me if I'm set on staying out West then to try and do what I can for Harrison.

The doctors say Har has a long road ahead of him. I decide I am not going to speak of this as I return to his bedside.

"My eye," Har says. "How am I going to look through a camera and set shots with a concussion and one eye?"

"I'll take care of it," I say.

"How?" Har says.

I don't know, but I know I am going to go to the set and try to do something.

* * *

Ocean Beach feels like a place that hasn't changed since the 1960s, or at least my idealized notions of it. Quiet. Plenty of surfers and longhairs going about their business. Nehru's trailers are parked across the street from the Blue Breaker Hotel near the pier and it stands out as very out of place.

I recognize Nehru from photos and television. Tall and thin, dressed in black with his trademark shock of rockabilly black hair gone salt and pepper. He's at the center of a posse of Hollywood types sitting in folding chairs. I don't like that there is trash and cigarette butts on the ground. They're watching an open fire hydrant gush water into the street.

"Harrison, who?" Nehru replies to me when I tell him I'm here for Har.

"Smoothie Boy," one of his people says.

"Oh yes, Smoothie Boy," Nehru says. "Speaking of which, we need smoothies. I'm going to have—"

"I don't get smoothies," I say.

"Then why are you here? What could you possibly—"

I go to my truck and retrieve a pipe wrench. It takes me less than two minutes to close the hydrant.

"I guess your location is back the way you need it and you can resume shooting. No need to thank me, this one's free."

Nehru and his staff watch for a moment then the back to work motions begin. No one thanks me. This was a failure. I turn back to my truck and find Nehru walking toward me.

"How long is your friend laid out for?"

"I don't know. A while."

"We wrap in two weeks. I need a script supervisor."

"Me? I have a job."

"Doing what?"

"A plumber."

"Of course. How much does that pay?"

I tell him.

"I'll give you that, per day. Here. Here's, one, two, three days in advance."

He takes hundred-dollar bills from a roll from his pocket and hands them to me.

"Get him the shooting scripts," he calls.

"What do I have to do?"

"What you did just there," he says. "Oh, and keep me on track. I'm so easily distracted."

"This doesn't sound fun. At all."

"It isn't. Listen, I say make yourself some fast money. Give it to your friend Smoothie Boy, or whatever, I don't care. If it all works out maybe you can give him a job yourself once he's back on his feet."

* * *

On my balcony I sort out the continuity of Nehru's film. I figure out a way he can finish the shoot in eight days not fourteen if he listens to me. I can't wait to tell Har when I visit him later.

The phone rings. I run inside and grab it. It's Chase. She's frantic. Through her cries she tells me Moon has overdosed.

I race to her place and find her waiting outside with a black plastic bag packed full of her stuff. Two cops are leaning against their cruiser writing a report.

"I'm outta here," Chase says. "Can I stay with you? I can't go back to this."

* * *

When I arrive at Har's room the nurse doesn't let me in; she tells me he doesn't want to see me. I pretend to leave and when she turns the corner on her rounds I bolt into the room.

"Get the fuck out of here," Har says. "I told them I don't want to see you."

"Har, what the hell is going on?"

"I asked you one thing." He hits the call button. "To take care of her. What do you do? You steal my girl. *And* you steal my fucking job."

"That is absolutely not what is going on—"

The nurse comes through the door and gets in between us.

"You have to leave, right now, sir."

I let her lead me out.

"I never want to see you again," Har calls after me. "Both of you. Ever again."

* * *

It's been months and Har has kept his promise. Six weeks ago, they moved him from the hospital to somewhere, I don't know where.

I wait for Chase to leave the apartment. She's off on a buy which means I've got three hours before she's back. Nehru's film wrapped early and under budget. The wrap party was a blast and I met a ton of Hollywood types; not all of them were assholes. We haven't heard from Moon but Chase apparently took her habit with her in the plastic bag.

I've got a film shoot lined up in LA and an apartment waiting in Venice Beach.

I leave Chase a note explaining that I can't live like this. Along with a copy of the lease. The keys. And enough cash to cover next month's rent. She's gonna blow it on smack but I did the right thing.

I make one last call. I get Har's answering machine. Just like every call for the last three months. As I pull away with everything I own in my truck I wonder what became of Moon. I'll never know. I'm pretty sure she told me her real name on the roof of the shower in the desert but for the life of me I cannot remember.

* * *

It is my first interview since being back in New York and I'm nervous about the call. I realize I haven't thought much of Chase and Moon and Har for years when the memory of them and the cloud rolling over us floods into me in response to the first question.

"You came out West for Rehab. Worked as a plumber. And were studying to go back to school all before your first film, is this true?"

"Mostly," I say. "*Beneath the Dark Snow of Winter* was my first job. It was a Nehru Casteltinni film."

"Nehru's film sets are notorious for the… indulgences. What was that like for you?"

"Well a magician doesn't give away all his tricks, I probably shouldn't say."

"You're not condoning drug use?"

"No, I'm not. Like everyone in LA, I do admit I had a time when that was me. Unlike everyone in LA, I personally didn't like that kind of life, with all due respect. That's why New York is home again. It's different for me here."

"What's the first thing you did coming back to New York? Besides making the movie and now opening the new Production studio. Hit up your favorite pizza place?"

"Ha, I wish. Yes, I love the pizza. But no, first thing I did was get clean, really clean. Second thing was pay off my parents' mortgage. If the Company goes the way I plan, third thing on my list is to buy them a summer home."

In my mind's eye I see the bottle connecting with Har's face and I can answer no further questions.

* * *

New York City, 2007

IT'S BEEN A ROUGH YEAR for film. I lost another production to a studio in New Zealand. A producer friend of mine told me how he went out with and slept with an actress we work with, an actress for whom I've held a candle for years. I have half a mind to take the rest of the year off.

I leave work early to grab a comic book on Bleeker street that I'm supposed to have read for a production. A woman walking down the stairs from the astrology shop above catches my eye.

"Chase? Is that you?"

Her hair is no longer that California blond. She's dyed it black and it's cut short and modern, but it is her.

"Wow, what are you doing here?"

"I was just going to ask the same of you," I say. "You're in New York?"

"Ten years now. I'm in banking. I work as a mortgage broker over in Union Square."

"Wait. My offices are in Union Square. Ten years and I've never seen you?"

"I work a lot," she says

"So do I."

"You clean? I'm clean."

"Yeah, me too," I say.

Bleeker Street is a flood of people. A thousand lives. A thousand stories passing by.

"I'm heading back up to 14th," she says. Want to walk?"

"Yeah sure."

She extends her arm the way Europeans do. I link mine in hers and it is nice.

"Hey. You ever hear from Harrison?"

"I used to," she says. "For a bit, on and off. I got tired of his shit."

"How was he?"

"Last I heard, he was a greeter at Walmart somewhere." She extends her lower lip and blows a strand of hair from her face. "Wow, this had to be over ten years ago."

A pang of guilt hits me over how attractive I find the unconscious little gesture.

"That's good? I guess…"

"He hated it. And so you don't have to ask, he still hated you. Don't feel bad, to be fair he hated everyone, even me. Most of all himself."

The sun is going down. Being in her company makes me think of how long it has been since I've seen the stars.

"What was it, twenty years ago, we were out in the desert? I always think of you all Thanksgiving time."

"Twenty?" she says. "Try more like fifteen, I'm not *that* old."

"You look great."

"Thanks, every year counts."

"I wish I had photos. I never developed Moon's camera. Sometimes I wish I had."

"That whore. Holy hell, I haven't thought of her in forever."

"Yeah, me too."

That's a lie. I can see Moon posing in front of the glowing cloud as if the glossy thick paper were in my hands before me.

We arrive at the street across from the Christmas shopping village set up in the park surrounding the Union Square subway stop.

"You off for the day?" I ask. "I mean, you want to go for Mexican food, or something?"

"In New York? You know that's impossible."

"True—"

"Last night I was thinking of my Dad and my abuela and I made tamales."

"How's your Dad?"

"In prison."

"I'm sorry."

"I'm not. I left him behind with California."

"Oh."

"And I swore to stop dating guys like him too."

"Tall dark and knowledgeable of all best drug plane routes? How's that going?"

"Don't ask," she says.

I wish she had laughed.

"Hey, you want to try the tamales I made? Not that you're qualified to know if they're any good."

"That would be perfect."

We find our way to the foot of the skyscraper that is hers. Her apartment is a couple of rooms high up. The living room and kitchen are a windowless rectangle. The door to her tiny box-sized bedroom is open; the space filled entirely by the bed. One wall is all window looking out into Manhattan's dusk.

I watch her put the tamales in the oven. Take out two fancy glasses and mix two drinks. There was a time when I'd never had Mexican food. Or a cocktail. Watching her is hypnotic. There's something on her mind she cannot mask. I remember how good she looked in the Photo-mat; tempered by the weight of things she's seen, her beauty is now much more profound.

"Which way to the restroom?" I ask.

"Other side of the apartment," she says.

I stand and shuffle through the dark. I stop at a doorway. There's a shape before me. My eyes, blurry from the dark, register that I'm looking in a mirror. But I'm in plumber's blue work clothes. I squint and for a second I think I'm seeing a younger visage of my dad. I move my hand to see if the image moves. Am I looking at myself?

I'm not looking at a mirror—five other man-sized apparitions appear in a row. I sense that they are all… me. I can not see clear enough to discern faces or clues from what they are wearing. I just… sense them; presences as real and true as the certainty when I know it is going to rain a few seconds before a cloudburst.

"Hey, not there, make a left," Chase calls.

I'm standing facing a wall. No mirror. No doorway.

I walk left. In the bathroom I feel throbbing aches in all the places I shot up long ago. My arms. My legs. Behind my knees. These pains are not real, I tell myself. Why now? Why do I want to use now? Why do I yearn for that oblivion? This call of the void is not real either, I tell myself. It has to be some kind of sadness. Some mournfulness for lives not lived.

"You were coming from that astrology place on Bleeker," I say as I take my place again on the couch. "How was it?"

"Oh, that?" she says and brings the drinks and sits next to me. "I was telling my friend not to worry, that I won't be coming round for a while. I don't believe in that shit anymore."

"Someone once told me the stars don't know or even care if you believe in them and their relationships or not."

"That's such bullshit," she says. "Please don't tell me you're into that."

"Do I look like I am?"

She answers by downing her drink. I follow suit. It's strong. I'm not used to alcohol and I can't not think of Har. Even after all these years I think of Chase as his girl and I have a pang of guilt for what we're about to do.

Seconds into our kiss I realize it is the best kiss of my life. Her lips are communicating something. This is reverse oblivion. My mind is full of a thousand things I want to tell her. My hands are in her hair. Then under her blouse and on her back. She's grasping at me as she leads me across the room.

"I want you. Now," she whispers then bites my ear. She pushes me onto her bed with a force that startles us to a halt.

I gently pull her to me and for a few minutes we lay together, breathing heavy, watching the last of the day in the sky.

"You ever think of the cloud?" I say.

"That thunderhead?"

"Yeah. That day you told me I'd never look at the sky the same way again. You remember?"

"No. Sounds like something I'd say. Was I right?"

"So right," I say under my breath. "Wish I was there now. We should just leave here and go."

"What are you whispering? If I did say it, I was so fucking kidding or high out of my mind. I never want to go back to California again. It can fall off into the ocean with the big quake for all I care."

She leans to kiss me, gently pulling me closer.

I think to speak up and ask her out loud and for real if she'll go back to the desert with me. I close my eyes and can feel her. One point in the night. Is it because the distance between us is so minute? Once the shape that was us was three-sided. And then four. Is it possible to feel that ever again? It is hard to believe in things. It is easy to spiral on, head down. On lighted paths, real for certain. Maybe Moon isn't dead and is out there somewhere. Maybe Har is going to speak with me again, someday.

I clear my throat to ask. The last light of the day is disappearing in the skyscraper-crowded sky. Instead of speaking, I press my lips to the sweet curve between her shoulder and neck and let her take me.

The Walking Man

AT FIRST I THOUGHT I'd start this by describing him as a sort of mad Colonel Kurtz, in reverse, a poet warrior, walking out of the jungle of Papua New Guinea to the four corners of Japan, into his own personal heart of light.

But that wouldn't do. Nor would any cryptic reference or word puzzle made up of his haiku. As much as this would please him. And then I thought maybe I'd begin with an image of the man behind the glass window, screaming, screaming, for people to hear, yet they are walking on by, oblivious to the workings of his mind, the strings of words stitched together from his heart.

I am one of them. A fool who mistook the etchings on the glass, the panes fogging with midnight breath, for the workings of a genius bored with the conventions of conventional prose.

"Love ignition overdrive," he reads to the crowd.

The words come alive in my mind. And I am enlightened to the mysteries of his zodiac.

We study and teach and plot in his Brisbane garden hideaway. We drink wine and feast on Thai food with friends in the shadow of the golden Buddha, knowing that this is but a moment. One of *those* moments, a wild convergence of so many lifelines that will never cross again. I see that mournful glint, ever present in his clear eyes. I deduce meanings and stories from the fragments of word-filled papers he carries, relics of moments, stretching into the past. I marvel at the giant pirate chest full of words he has amassed.

And I think of him, walking. Into the future, a line stretching away from our intersected moments, strung from his treasury of words.

I'd thought I'd write about a man who walked and walked and transformed all he saw into immortal art in the pattern of the ancients. In this story he doesn't stop. He keeps on walking. Through all of Japan. All of Asia. All the world. And up into space, rising in a swell of mystic rhythms and notes, free from the iPod full of acid jazz and punk rock tethering him to the ground.

He walks from planet to planet. Footsteps dissolving into sprays of cosmic dust. Every expression cosmically significant, yet meaning nothing at all.

His treasure chest, no longer needed, left earthbound.

A Picture of Zurich

I AM SEVENTEEN. The store in our town that sells prints and lithographs is going out of business. On the evening of my departing for university, I find myself shopping there and a print of a city on a lake, framed by mountains, captures me.

The image is comprised of tiny squares. Bright oranges. Cobalt blues and silvers for the lake. Forty dollars is the final price, after many reductions and cross outs marked on a sticker tag on the back. I paid what was then a tidy sum and took the picture with me to university.

* * *

The picture stays with me wherever I live. For a decade it adorns my walls in a simple, silver frame, then spends the next ten years rolled up in a storage tube.

* * *

I am thirty-seven. Stepping foot on Zurich's paving-stone streets for the first time, memories of my almost-forgotten print flood back to me. My business in Zurich is done and with a day on my hands before having to return to the States, I change out of my suit and tie into sneakers and comfortable jeans.

The air is clean and it is something about the pace, the rhythm of all the people, and not just the river and ring of mountains that makes me feel like the painting.

I wind past clock towers and churches. Cafés are setting up tables for lunch with care and grace. The shops sell exquisite paper, artists tools, beautiful furniture, absinthe, coffee, and of course chocolate. I am lost but I don't care. I am wandering.

I enter a shop. A dozen paintings hang on its walls. Each is in the style of my Zurich print but each is of the cities I have lived in. A man is at an artist's work desk cutting squares of paper, tools neatly laid out in front of him. He turns and his face is mine—bearded and gray, but mine nonetheless.

Everything disappears. The shop is empty. I go back outside and notice an elegant for sale sign in the window. I wander a while and find my way back to my hotel but I know I won't be returning to the States anytime soon. I realize why I have come.

PRESIDENT · 1917 · 1926
HOUDI
WEISS

Houdini's Grave

I'M STANDING OUTSIDE STARBUCKS on 2nd Avenue, and a woman with long dark hair called my name from across the street as if she knew me. She dashed over when the traffic passed and said, "Sorry I'm late. I hope I haven't kept you waiting too long. It's so nice to meet you." She had my name right, but she was obviously there for a blind date with another man. My fortune cookie at lunch had said, "opportunity knocks" so I figured this was it, so we went inside. Then we walked, hot cocoa in hand, laughing at the storefronts already decorated for Halloween. We ended up in a cozy Irish pub.

I've been on more than my share of bad dates but things were going amazingly right. So right that I forgot it was all just a mistake. She was a painter. Did charity exhibitions of her work for projects in South America. It wasn't just that she was tall and stylish with that long, dark hair, though that wasn't hurting; the way she spoke made me want to listen and gave me a sense of future. I found myself feeling oddly mournful that we hadn't met years ago. I wanted our story to start now, like I felt it was, so I had to come clean.

"I'm not the guy you were supposed to meet," I said.

"Of course you are," she said.

She didn't get it. Then she asked me if I was doing anything on Halloween. I had a ticket to the Police concert in Madison Square Garden. She said a friend of hers was a famous magician and a few of them were gathering at Houdini's grave.

"The ultimate escape artist," she said and then she talked as if she knew me for ages. About an abusive husband. A controlling ex-boyfriend. A small part of me said this is too much too fast and that her fascination with Houdini was an ominous metaphor. A trapped woman looking for the first lockpick that comes along. But I didn't listen. It had started to rain and she insisted on driving me to my car.

"I'd love to go to Houdini's grave with you on Halloween," I said.

"Sure?" she asked. "It's at midnight."

"Absolutely."

She wrote her number on a Starbucks napkin and gave me a peck goodnight.

Our conversation continued on the phone the next evening. We stayed up late into the night, ending the conversation after she gave me directions to the grave. The next night I wasn't able to reach her. Nor the night after. And the night after.

Two weeks passed without word. I agonized about going to the graveyard or not and now, standing here, alone in the wet cold waiting for midnight to come, I wonder if she was a figment of my imagination. Or if she got in touch with the man she was supposed to meet that night.

I think of going to find her, I have her card, then decide that's dangerously close to stalking.

Turning my back to the wind, I realize she's out there; an instance of the potential of the situation being much safer than reality. I don't want her to turn out to be an invented ghost.

But I have to know. So I steel myself against the October night, hoping this isn't where the story ends but where it gets good.

Acknowledgements

Thank you to my friends and colleagues and the editors and publishers who helped bring these stories to their initial publications: Justin Burnett, Scott J. Couturier, Matt Cowan, Rudi Dornemann, Tom English, Chris Karr, Shayne Keene, Duane Pesice, and Sarah Walker.

To Dan Sauer for his vision, talent, and dedication to art and the written word. Working with him makes it all a great joy.

My most heartfelt thank you, as always, to my family.

About the Author

DANIEL BRAUM writes short stories that explore the tension between the psychological and the supernatural. His debut short story collection *The Night Marchers and Other Strange Tales* (2016) was re-released in 2023 in a new edition from Cemetery Dance Publications with a cover by Dan Sauer. He intentionally adopts the term "strange tales" for his stories in homage to author Robert Aickman and the intentional ambiguities of his work.

His short fiction can be found in his collections *Underworld Dreams* (2020) from Lethe Press, the illustrated chapbook *Yeti Tiger Dragon* (2016) from Dim Shores, and *The Wish Mechanics* (2017) from Independent Legions. His collection *Phantom Constellations* is forthcoming from Cemetery Dance Publications in Fall 2025. His stories have also appeared in places ranging from the *The Best Horror of the Year Volume 12* edited by Ellen Datlow and *Shivers 8* edited by Richard Chizmar to *Lady Churchill's Rosebud Wristlet* and many anthologies. Braum first worked with Dan Sauer in the pages of *The Audient Void: A Journal of Weird Fiction and Dark Fantasy*.

His novella *The Serpent's Shadow* was released in trade paperback by Cemetery Dance in Fall 2023. His novel *Servant of the Eighth Wind* is forthcoming from Lethe Press. He is the host of the New York Ghost Story Festival and the Night Time Logic reading series.

Find him at bloodandstardust.wordpress.com

About the Artist

DAN SAUER is a graphic designer and artist living in Oregon. In 2016, he co-founded (with editor/publisher Obadiah Baird) *The Audient Void: A Journal of Weird Fiction and Dark Fantasy*, which features his design and illustration work. Since 2017, he has worked extensively on book covers, interior art and custom lettering for Hippocampus Press, Centipede Press, and other publishers. His art often takes the form of surreal collage and photomontage, as pioneered by artists such as Max Ernst, Wilfried Sätty, Harry O. Morris and J. K. Potter.

Publication History

"Where the Jaguar King Lives in the Dark Heart of the Wood" first appeared in *Nightmare Abbey* #5 (2024), edited by Tom English.

"A Loch Ness Monster Under the Light of the Southern Cross" first appeared in *A Darkness Visible* (2023), edited by Justin Burnett.

"Phantom Constellations" is original to this publication.

"Human Impersonation Day" first appeared in *Weird Fiction Quarterly* (2024), edited by Scott Couturier, Chris Karr, Shayne Keen, and Sarah Walker.

"Kookaburra," "Breathstealer," "Go.", "Boon of the Monkey God," "Matthias and the Sentinel," The Moalai," "On Darkened Lawns," "In Search of Elephant Corners," "The Walking Man," "A Picture of Zurich," and "Houdini's Grave" first appeared in the *Daily Cabal* between the years 2008 and 2011.

DIABOLIC DARKNESS IN THE SONORAN DESERT

"Imagine Arkham relocated to the desert southwest and rebuilt on a foundation of Mexican-American mythology, folklore, language, and spirituality. That will give you some idea of what lies in store for you in the pages of *The Burning Ember Mission of Helldorado* . . ."

—**Rebecca Buchanan**, author of *Asphalt Gods* and *Not a Princess, but (Yes) There was a Pea, and Other Fairy Tales to Foment Revolution*

THE BURNING EMBER MISSION OF HELLDORADO

In this decadent collection, Manuel Arenas relates a series of Southwestern Gothic tales told from the perspective of the Latin diaspora. In the title novelette—a supernatural conte cruel—we meet the sardonic Ba'al Adrian Zwartenberg, a sorcerer seeking to resurrect an abandoned beacon of evil—and who delights in horrific revenge for the slightest offense. The poems and stories that follow feature other dark icons from Arenas' Southwestern mythology: Lupe of the mirror black—a *tlahuelpuchi* (vampiric shapeshifter); the tragic Altagracia (who inherits a family curse); the demonic *brujo* Dimas Akelarre; and Féretrina, aka Coffin-belly Mary—an emissary for La Santa Muerte.

ILLUSTRATED BY MUTARTIS BOSWELL

AVAILABLE NOW FROM

JACKANAPES PRESS

www.JackanapesPress.com
www.facebook.com/Jackanapes-Press